The sk_____ over the
highest _____ ok a sharp
turn. A _____ ur of its bird-of-prey
prow. Th_____ caught fire, swerved, and went
off the edge of the cliff. The screams of the men
inside could be heard as they plummeted to their
deaths.

Pythias stood watching the carnage in horror, jaw
agape. He waited for the last car to be destroyed. It
was sufficiently far behind the others so that the driver
was able to stop.

The men got out and started running back down the
road—all but one of them.

One by one, the four fleeing men were vaporized by
the laser fire. Only one remained alive now looking
up at the skyfighter.

Waiting for him to be killed, Pythias was amazed to
see the skyfighter move away from the cliff, out over
the ocean, and vanish, without firing a single shot at
the lone man.

Even from here, Pythias knew who he was . . .

Other V books from Pinnacle

V

THE NEW ENGLAND RESISTANCE

Tim Sullivan

PINNACLE BOOKS NEW YORK

V: THE NEW ENGLAND RESISTANCE

An original Pinnacle Books edition, published for the first time
anywhere.

First printing/June 1985

ISBN: 0-523-42467-1
Can. ISBN: 0-523-43442-1

Printed in the United States of America

PINNACLE BOOKS, INC.
1430 Broadway
New York, New York 10018

9   8   7   6   5   4   3   2   1

For Mike Dirda

THE
NEW ENGLAND
RESISTANCE

Chapter 1

Though it was still late afternoon, the shadows in Mike's Tavern were deep around the booths and tables where lobstermen and hunters drank. Everyone, the bartender included, looked up warily as the front door opened.

A man entered, squinted in the darkness, and walked to the last booth.

"John," he said. "John Ellis, is that you?"

"Ayuh," a deep voice answered. "What can I do you for, Phil?"

"There's a stranger just got off the bus."

"Lots of strangers come to Cutter's Cove, especially in the fall. Good huntin'."

"Not like this guy. He's asking about Dr. Brunk."

Nobody spoke for a long moment. Then there were the sounds of heavy boots and rifle stocks rubbing against the hardwood floor as the men put down their drinks and rose.

"Where is he?" John Ellis asked.

"Walking down Union Street toward Main, last I saw him."

Ellis led the way, blond hair streaming under his hunter's cap, his bulk filling the doorway. Outside, the men slipped shells into their guns and checked the safeties, somewhat sobered by the salt air. They clomped along the wooden sidewalk until they came to the corner.

The ocean came into sight, crumbling piers and a

1

V

cannery along the shore. On Main Street walked a solitary man.

"Hey!" John Ellis cried. "You!"

The man looked up at them. He appeared to be in his thirties, thin, with a big nose and a worried, furrowed brow. As they came toward him, he didn't run as they expected. He just stopped walking and stood his ground.

In a moment he was surrounded by the armed mob. Fifteen men watched him closely as their spokesman questioned him.

"What are you doing around here?" Ellis demanded.

"Doing?" The stranger's accent was odd. "I'm lurching for Dr. Randall Brunk."

"Huh? Lurching? You mean *searching* for Dr. Brunk?"

"Yes, searching. That is correct. Can you help me find him?"

Ellis ignored him. "Where you from?" he asked.

"Los Angeles."

Sizing up the man's windbreaker, trousers, and polished shoes, John Ellis said, "You look too normal to come from L.A."

"Nevertheless, that is where—"

Ellis grabbed him roughly by the collar. "Let's get a closer look at your face."

The stranger didn't struggle as two men gripped his arms from behind.

"George," said John Ellis, "hold my rifle."

The man took his gun, and Ellis turned back to the stranger. "Now let's see what you're made out of."

He reached toward the thin face and clutched the loose skin just under the jawbone and pulled. The skin stretched an inhuman length and snapped free, a two-inch-long piece still in Ellis' hand.

Where the skin had been on the stranger's face, there

was now a long, jagged rip along the jaw. Green, scaly flesh was revealed, but the stranger still didn't flinch.

His manner affected the men strangely. In the past, they had always been boisterous when they caught a Visitor, but they were silent now.

"I am not your enemy," the alien said.

"Shoot, of course you ain't," one of the men in the crowd said. "You're just like us."

"If you aren't our enemy," John Ellis said, "who is?"

"I admit that my people are your enemies," the Visitor said, "but I am not. I have come to help Dr. Brunk."

"Help him? From what we hear, he's working on a new poison to finish you lizards off once and for all. Why would you want to help him?"

The Visitor tried to say more, but he was drowned out by the shouts of the men, who pulled him forward roughly. As they dragged him toward the courthouse, faces peered out of windows and cracked doors at the spectacle passing by.

At the courthouse, a rope was strung over a brick arch. A bigger crowd began to gather as a wooden crate was set under the makeshift gallows and the Visitor was lifted up onto it with the noose around his neck. The people shouted for his blood.

"Well, Mr. Lizard," John Ellis shouted over the din, "you got a name?"

"I am called Willie," the Visitor said, scales glistening green where his human pseudo skin had been torn away.

"Willie, say your prayers—if you heathens have such a thing as prayers."

A burly man approached the crate with the intention of kicking it away, but at that moment Willie began to chant something in the alien tongue, a rasping, melodic sound not of this earth.

The crowd was silenced, transfixed. The strange chanting was unlike anything they had ever heard before, and yet it was plainly of a spiritual nature . . . a very highly developed spiritual nature, at that.

The song ended as abruptly as it had begun, and the people were moved in spite of themselves. A few even returned to their clapboard houses before the hanging, wanting no part of it.

"All right," John Ellis said, regaining his sense of command, "he's said his prayers. Wilbur, kick that crate over."

The burly man raised his leg.

Willie was silent.

Everyone waited for the end, but with none of the blood lust they had felt a few moments ago.

A shot rang out, thundering out over the ocean and echoing through the town.

"Kick that crate over, Wilbur," a voice said, "and you're a dead man."

Chapter 2

A gray-bearded, grizzled old man stepped through the crowd with a shotgun leveled at the would-be hangman.

"Kick that box, son, and there'll be two dead men here."

Wilbur stepped back, hands outstretched in supplication. He disappeared into the crowd.

"What the hell you think you're doing here, Pythias?" John Ellis demanded.

"What do you think *you're* doing here, John Ellis?" the old man said accusingly. "I know your father taught you better than to string a man up without giving him a fair trial."

"This isn't a man, Pythias. Look at him."

Pythias Day glanced at Willie. "I see him."

The shotgun remained leveled at John Ellis.

"Dammit, Pythias, you know what his kind have done to our people."

"Stringing him up," Pythias Day observed, "won't make you any better than the Visitors. In fact, I'd say it puts you right in the same league with 'em."

The crowd murmured its agreement.

"Take him down," Pythias Day instructed.

John Ellis hesitated for a few seconds and then nodded toward one of his followers. The man jumped up on the crate and quickly removed the noose from Willie's neck.

Willie stepped down onto the ground and looked into

the eyes of Pythias Day. He saw no softness in the man, only a concern for justice. "Thank you," he said.

"Don't thank me yet. You still got some explaining to do, mister."

"Of course," Willie said, then explained that he had come searching for Dr. Brunk, as he had told the others.

"What for?" Pythias Day asked suspiciously.

"I am to be a control in an experiment involving a new toxin."

"A control? If I hear you right, you're saying you came here as a . . . a guinea pig."

Willie remained silent.

"Well, if that's the truth, I reckon we're all gonna owe you a big apology. And if you ain't telling the truth, we'll know soon enough."

"How are we gonna find out?" John Ellis asked.

"If you weren't so damn hotheaded, John," said Pythias, "you'd of figured it out by yourself." He frowned at the younger man. "I'm gonna take him over to Brunk's and see if there's any truth in what he says."

"And what if he's some kind of spy?"

"Well, he already knows what Doc's up to out at that lab, so he won't learn any new secrets. And if he's lying, we'll put him in a cell, same as anybody else suspected of committing a crime."

"You talk like you're the sheriff," Ellis sneered.

"The mayor swore me in yesterday, John. I guess you were too busy drinking to know what's been going on since Sheriff Evans was killed last week."

Ellis glared at him for a moment and then looked down at his boots. "All right, Pythias, you win."

The old man slapped Ellis's shoulder. "It's a good man who can admit he's wrong," he said sincerely.

"You gonna need any help taking this buzzard out to Brunk's?" Ellis asked.

"Naw, I'll be okay."

The crowd dispersed, except for Ellis and Pythias Day and their captive. Finally, Ellis shrugged and walked away.

Day gestured with his shotgun, and Willie started in the indicated direction.

A few hundred yards later, they came to a white Victorian house replete with gingerbread trimmings and a big front porch. There was a jeep parked in the yard.

Day pointed at the jeep, and Willie got in. Day sat in the driver's seat and fished in his coat pocket until he came up with a key. He started the jeep and backed out of the yard. As they drove up Main Street, Day asked Willie what his name was.

Willie told him, and then said, "Thank you for saving my life."

"Might not have saved you," Day replied. "Might have just put off your execution by a few days."

"You will soon know the truth," Willie said with certainty.

"One way or the other."

Pythias Day drove a winding two-lane road between immense glacial boulders as if he had done it a thousand times, which he had. Willie admired the scenery. He found Earth very beautiful, though much of the natural beauty had been destroyed by man himself. Still, there was no chance of Earth regaining her grandeur if all her water was taken. It was simply not morally defensible to drain a world of its life's blood, even if it was to save your own planet.

"You were pretty cool standing up on that crate," Pythias said. "Seemed like you weren't afraid to die."

"When it is time for one's spirit to leave one's body, one must resign oneself to the end. However, the *preta-na-ma* teaches that there is no real end."

"The *preta-na*-what?" Day asked, taking a hairpin curve at sixty miles an hour.

"The *preta-na-ma*. It is an ancient system of belief, forbidden now on my planet."

"Well, I'll allow you derive some strength from it, whatever it is."

The jeep sped over the top of a cliff, the ocean sparkling below like an eternity of gems. A few minutes later they reached the cliff's highest point, a flat area with an expansive view of the sea and much of Cutter's Cove as well as the island off the coast. Pythias pulled his jeep into a small parking lot—empty in the middle of the afternoon—adjoining a cluster of long, one-story, white-washed buildings. He cut the engine and sat staring at the quiet structures.

"Brunk Laboratories, Willie," he said. "But it don't look like anybody's home."

Chapter 3

"Perhaps the resistance was not the only force to learn of Dr. Brunk's work," Willie said.

Day stroked his beard, looking at Willie as if trying to figure out if the alien was second-guessing him with that comment. "You might be right," he said at length. "Let's go take a look."

They got out of the jeep and walked toward the laboratory complex. Except for the whipping of the salt wind and the crying of gulls, the place was completely still. Day held his shotgun like a newborn babe, stroking the outside of the finger guard as he walked. He did not point the gun at Willie, perhaps sensing that if there was action now, Willie would not be his target.

They peered in the windows lining the lab walls. There was no sign of life inside, only long rows of tables and sinks, shelves of glassware, and locked doors.

"This is the damnedest thing I ever saw," Pythias opined. "But I'm beginning to wonder if it's more than a coincidence that you're here the day this place turns into a ghost town."

"I have told you all I know," Willie insisted. "The resistance has sent me here to work with Dr. Brunk."

"Did they send word you were coming?"

"I believe so."

"Then maybe somebody else got that message," Pythias said. "Your people have a way of closing down scientific establishments."

"That is true, but I don't think that is the case here."

"Why not?" Pythias reached in his hunting jacket pocket and withdrew a packet of chewing tobacco. He bit off a healthy plug and then offered some to Willie.

Willie declined, thanking him before he explained his reasoning. "This compound was closed in an orderly fashion, without any resistance. I believe that the people who lurk here left willingly, suspecting that my people are on the way."

"How come you didn't know this before, Willie?" Pythias eyed him sourly.

"I have been traveling incognito, on a bus from Boston since early this morning. This was done so no suspicion would be aroused at the various checkpoints along the way. I received no messages from the resistance since I left Los Angeles."

Pythias mulled that over for a few seconds. "Makes sense," he said at last. "And you know what else makes sense, Willie?"

Willie shook his head.

"That we better get out of here. Because those Visitors might be closing in on this place right now."

"I'm afraid it's too late," Willie said, his brow furrowed.

"Huh?" Pythias stared into Willie's blue eyes, but the alien wasn't looking at him. He was looking past him at the sky. Pythias slowly turned and saw something he had hoped he'd never see again after the last skirmish a few days before, in which the previous sheriff was killed. It was a Visitor skyfighter, hovering at the cliff's edge.

"Goddammit," Pythias muttered. He turned to see if there was anyplace to run to, but several red-clad Visitors without their human disguises, were coming out of the bushes around the premises. All of them held laser pistols, pointing them straight at Pythias and Willie.

"Willie, I hope I'm facing death with the courage you showed this afternoon." With that, Pythias leveled the shotgun at the nearest Visitor and fired, knocking the alien off his feet.

The downed Visitor sat up, the birdshot absorbed by his protective vest. Pythias calmly broke open the shotgun and popped in another shell. Pulling up the barrel, he took aim and fired again, blasting a second alien off his feet. This continued until he loaded his last shell. However, the Visitors kept advancing as their ship landed in the parking lot.

Pythias fired the last round, frustrated that he hadn't killed one of his assailants but satisfied that at least he was going down fighting.

"That will be enough, Mr. Day," said a big Visitor standing on the skyfighter ramp. "Put down your weapon."

"The hell I will." Pythias turned the shotgun around and held it as if it were a baseball bat. "Come on and get what's coming to you, you slimy lizards." He looked at Willie. "No offense intended."

"None taken." Willie stepped forward and addressed the Visitor captain. "Don't harm this man," he said. "He will be of more use to you alive than dead."

Pythias glaced at Willie, long white wisps of hair streaming in the breeze. "And I was beginning to believe in you," he shouted, rushing at Willie and trying to strike him with the gun butt.

Half a dozen Visitor claws grasped at the old man, rendering him helpless by tearing the gun from his hands. He cursed them and shouted at them as they took him away.

The alien leader walked imperiously down the ramp. He spoke to Willie in their own tongue, the tongue of the *preta-na-ma* corrupted by rampant militarism and cruelty. "Who are you?" he demanded.

Remembering that the local sheriff had been killed only a week before, Willie guessed that there had been much fighting in this area. "They took me prisoner a few days ago," he said.

"How many days?"

"I don't know," Willie replied. "I was locked up in the darkness for a long time."

The captain gazed at him through his dark glasses. "You will stay with us until a skyfighter leaves for the Mother Ship. Until then your loyalty is to me."

Willie bowed. "What is our mission here?"

The captain's reptilian lips curled up in pleasure. "To find a human who goes by the name of Dr. Randall Brunk."

Chapter 4

Willie didn't know how long he could fool Ronald, the captain. Indeed, he wasn't sure Ronald was fooled; he might have only been pretending to believe Willie's story, biding his time until he could learn more about the resistance.

Willie had to get away as soon as possible, and he was obliged to help Pythias Day escape too. After all, the man wouldn't be here now had he not saved Willie's life from the mob back in Cutter's Cove.

Luckily, Pythias had not been taken aboard the skyfighter. He was locked in a small storage room—a large closet, really—in one of the laboratory buildings. The compound had been taken over so that a search could be made for any information about the new toxin. Brunk Laboratories would serve as a command center for the occupation of the Maine coast as well. Its computers would be like a nervous system for the Visitors' forces while they were here, a communications network second to none in this part of New England. Ronald had seen to that.

He pointed this all out to Willie as they walked through the largest of the lab buildings, occasionally jabbing toward points of interest with his laser pistol.

"How many would you estimate are in the local resistance?" Ronald suddenly asked.

Willie wasn't prepared for such an abrupt about-face. "Uh, a few dozen, I think."

"You think? It is your duty to observe the activities of

the enemy while you are in captivity. Surely, as a loyal member of our species you were aware of that?"

"Of course. There are about forty active resistance fighters." Willie was exaggerating for the sake of deterring any plans for attacking the villagers that Ronald might have been hatching. "And there are many more in the militia—a few hundred, I should think."

Ronald was silent, thinking that over. Doubtless this was a much larger number than he had anticipated. If he believed Willie, he would have to revise his plans.

"If they should mobilize their forces," he said, "they might be able to take this position from us. We can't have that."

Willie suddenly realized that the false information he was giving Ronald could lead to a drastic increase in Visitor forces.

"Of course, the resistance here believes it has success-fully repulsed the occupation, so they are quite lax right at the moment."

"Ah, I see." Ronald seemed pleased.

Willie had apparently helped prevent a direct attack on Cutter's Cove by overstating the size of the resistance, and circumvented the problem of more Visitor troops at the same time—at least for the moment. Still, he could have caused a lot of trouble if luck hadn't been with him.

Ronald gestured toward the storage room where Pythias Day was imprisoned. "You have told me more in a few moments than we have been able to get out of that wizened ape even under torture."

Willie hoped that his horror wouldn't show. His plan to help Pythias escape acquired new urgency now that he knew they were torturing the old man. He had assumed they would resort to such means, but not so quickly. These New England people were tough, so Ronald took extraordinary measures. Or did he merely enjoy torture for its own sake? Willie had known such sadists before,

and he didn't relish the idea of Ronald turning on him.
The Visitor captain seemed to believe that Willie was one
of them, so the time to act was now, before Ronald
changed his mind.

"Perhaps I could talk to the prisoner," Willie said.

"I was considering saving him for the conversion
process," mused Ronald. "But it might not be a bad idea
to let you talk to him."

"Yes, I believe he was growing quite attached to me
before your timely arrival. These humans are such
sentimental creatures, you know."

"And yet he seemed to blame you for his capture.
Still, he must understand that you are one of us, even if
he did keep you as a slave."

"Precisely."

"Very odd beings, but please try to reason with the
human."

Ronald instructed a guard to unlock the storage-room
door, and Willie entered. It was dark inside, and Pythias
squinted into the unexpected light from the doorway.

"What the hell do you want?" Pythias spat.

"Just to talk to you."

A light was brought in, and the door was closed.
Willie waited a moment and then moved closer to
Pythias, whispering, "I want to help you."

"You can help me by getting out of here." Pythias
turned his face to the wall.

"I didn't lead them here," Willie said. "Surely you
must realize that."

Pythias' face was fierce. "I don't know anything of the
kind. All I know is that before you came, we were
holding our own against the Visitors and they didn't have
any idea what Doc Brunk was doing up here. Now the
place is crawling with 'em."

Willie would never be able to convince him that he
was not the enemy until he actually made an attempt to

free him. He considered how this might be done, commended his spirit to Zon, sighed, and rose.

The door opened after Willie tapped on it. A bored guard stood without, waiting for Willie to step outside so the door could be locked.

Willie charged at the guard, his head down, butting him right in the midriff.

Chapter 5

The guard crashed into a shelf, glassware falling and shattering on the concrete floor. His laser pistol clattered amid the tinkling glass, and Willie scooped it up. He turned to Pythias.

"Run!" he shouted.

Pythias scrambled out of the closet with surprising agility for a man of his age. There were shouts as he joined Willie.

"I'm sorry I doubted you," he said.

Willie handed him the laser. "Go!" he cried.

Pythias ran for the door, a blue bolt of laser fire singeing his hair. Willie turned and faced the rushing guards as Pythias fumbled with the knob. In a moment he was outside, the clean salt air in his lungs as he darted for the jeep still parked in the lot where he had left it. He saw only two red uniforms in the way. They hadn't spotted him yet, so he stood a good chance if he could work the laser.

Pointing it at the nearest of them, he squeezed the trigger. The Visitor was hit squarely in the back, clawed hand reaching for the hole burned through his body as he went down. His cries alerted his companion, who stared in amazement as Pythias rushed toward him. He tried to take aim, but Pythias fired a second burst. The Visitor went down as the beam pierced his brain.

Pythias was at the jeep in seconds. He jumped in as an energy bolt scored the jeep's body, burning his hand.

17

Ducking down in the driver's seat, Pythias searched for the extra key hidden under the mat.

Another beam struck the jeep, narrowly missing the left front tire. If they got a tire, he was sunk. He found the key and raised it to the ignition. It seemed to take forever to fit it into the tiny slot. He glanced up to see a wall of red uniforms running across the parking lot toward him. They would close in on him in seconds.

The key went into the ignition. He turned it, shoved the gearshift into reverse, and squealed backward out of the parking lot, turning as he went.

Laser beams flew past him, one igniting the dry needles of a Scotch pine as he zigzagged down the narrow cliffside road. As he rounded the bend, he knew he was out of sight. They would undoubtedly send the skyfighter after him, but if he could just beat them down the cliff, he knew some dirt roads through woods so overgrown they would never get a shot at him.

He was driving so fast now that every bump sent the jeep leaping off all four tires. Braking only when he came to a curve, Pythias came close to plunging off the road to his death into the sea below several times. Somehow, he managed to stay on the road, his white-knuckled hands clutching the wheel with grim determination. He was better than halfway down to sea level when a shadow passed over the jeep.

Blue beams sent up showers of rock and gravel, some of it raining down on Pythias' head. He wished that he had a helmet, but he supposed his head was hard enough.

Reaching a straightaway, he gunned the engine. The beams were firing all around him, the skyfighter almost directly overhead.

Somehow he made it down to sea level, big rocks on either side of him as he bounced and hurtled along at a desperate speed.

A dazzling burst of light blinded him, and when he could see again he swerved to keep the jeep on the road. The plastic on the dashboard was bubbling, melted from the laser blast that had come within inches of killing him.

He could see the woods ahead. If he could just keep them guessing for a few more seconds. . . .

The laser fire seemed to redouble itself. Blue beams rained down around him as he rode a gauntlet of death. Suddenly he heard a bang, and the jeep began to careen wildly. A tire had been hit, blown out. Pythias pressed his foot to the floor, and the brakes squealed.

But he couldn't bring the jeep under control on this bumpy road. It pitched over on its side, and Pythias was tossed into the air.

Another laser beam hit the jeep, this time burning through to the gas tank. The jeep exploded in a tremendous sunburst, detritus flying in every direction. A huge plume of smoke boiled over the wreckage, obscuring the skyfighter from Pythias' sight.

He had landed in a blueberry thicket, scratched but not much the worse for wear. He got to his feet, tested his limbs, and ran the last few yards to the woods.

The forest's nurturing darkness enveloped him as he ran. He paused only to glance briefly behind him.

The skyfighter had landed on the gravel embankment next to the road, and the ramp was extending from its side now. In a moment the place would be crawling with Visitors.

Pythias moved deeper into the woods. The fire crackled behind him, and he heard the shouts of the creatures who were hunting him, strange, rasping voices speaking in an unknown tongue.

It was that very alienness that would save him now. He had lived sixty-seven years in these parts, and these woods were like second nature to him. They would never find him in here.

Sweat streaming from his brow, breathing labored, Pythias Day moved deeper into the woods, the sounds of the Visitors growing faint in the distance.

Chapter 6

Willie was pushed to his knees before Ronald, who stared down at him imperiously.

"Why did you betray my trust?" Ronald demanded.

"He saved my life when his people would have killed me," Willie said. "I felt that I had to do the same for him."

"And what of your own people, Willie? Did you feel nothing about your own?"

"We are wrong to make war on the Terrans," Willie said.

A guard pushed his face into the floor.

"Enough of that!" Ronald commanded. "I would hear what he has to say."

"But, Captain . . ."

"Silence." Ronald looked down at Willie. "Continue."

"By the teachings of Amon," Willie said, "the precepts of the *preta-na-ma*, our conduct on Earth is forbidden."

"But it is the *preta-na-ma* that is forbidden. And as for Amon, he is in exile, no better than a common criminal."

"You know that is not true," Willie said.

"I, a simple soldier? How would I know any more than I am taught?"

"The truth cannot so easily be suppressed," Willie said. "For a time, we might continue as we have been, taking much and giving little. But that is a corrupt way, and it will eventually destroy us from within."

"So you are a philosopher, are you?" said Ronald. "Then I shall concoct a fittingly philosophical punishment for you, my friend. But it will require a little thought."

Willie looked up at Ronald's cruel, serpentine features.

"Take him away," Ronald commanded the guards.

A rowboat cut slowly through the water in the late afternoon sun. Two people were aboard, a young woman and a middle-aged, bearded man. The man clutched a valise tightly while the woman rowed. They made their way between the rocks off a heavily wooded island and hopped out, unmindful of the cold surf on their feet as they pulled the boat onto the sandy shore.

"The cabin's up this way, Sarah," the man said.

The girl, pretty but businesslike, followed him into the woods. They walked for over an hour and then emerged into a clearing. A little cabin sat bathed in the shafting sunlight.

"Why did you build it away from the water?" Sarah asked.

"To protect it from nor'easters," the man said. "Those trees form a natural windbreak, and provide privacy."

The woman nodded. "It'll make it harder for them to spot it."

"Even from the air, it's not easy to see."

They walked up to the cabin, and the man pulled open the groaning door.

"It wasn't locked?" Sarah asked.

"No need for that out here. Besides, there's nothing to steal inside anyway."

They went in, and the man searched for lanterns.

When he found one, he struck a match and lit it. "Still plenty of oil in this one," he said absently. "And there's enough wood for a fire here, at least for tonight. We'll chop more in the morning."

Sarah nodded, watching him carefully unwrap the string sealing the valise. When he had it open, he withdrew a pouch. Opening that, he took out five tiny vials and set them on a rough wooden table.

"There they are," he said, "the last hope of mankind."

"If only we'd had time to test them on the Visitor volunteer," Sarah said. "We can't know for certain it's going to work, Dr. Brunk."

"No, not for certain." Dr. Randall Brunk turned toward a plastic-covered window and looked out at the woods. "But it's the only chance we have to defeat them."

He went to the table, slumping into an ancient chair next to it, from which rose a cloud of dust. His face drew near the vials of clear liquid. "All that work, and this is all we have to show for it," he said. "Three bottles of the toxin, and two bottles of the antidote. But if I'm right, we have the power right here in our hands to stop the Visitors once and for all."

He gathered up the vials and put them back in their pouch.

"If they hadn't warned us on time, though, all our work would have been in vain."

"Well," said Sarah, "we're here now, and the resistance has been alerted. There's nothing we can do but wait it out."

Dr. Brunk sighed. "We've come so far, too far to be thwarted now, Sarah."

"You're tired. Why don't you rest awhile? I'll walk back to the beach and see that the boat's well hidden while you're asleep."

"Thank you, dear."

Sarah went out, and Dr. Brunk closed his eyes, trying to sleep. But in the darkness, he seemed to see reptilian shapes leering, taunting him. He had spent his life as a chemist, working for the good of mankind. And now the Visitors had forced him to use his knowledge to create a substance to destroy Earth's enemies. And, God help him, he could only pray that it would work.

Chapter 7

"I should have never let him go," John Ellis murmured angrily into his beer.

"Couldn't really stop him, John," said Wilbur Grogan. "It was his decision."

"I could have stopped him." Ellis lifted his glass and drained it in a few quick gulps. "Better get a few men and look for him and that lizard." His face darkened at the mention of Willie.

Ellis rose from the booth and walked to the bar to pay Mike Sherman, the owner and bartender of Mike's Tavern, the only drinking establishment in town.

"John," Sherman said, "maybe you oughtn't jump to any conclusions. Pythias is a funny old bird, you know. Just because he hasn't put in an appearance since this afternoon don't necessarily mean something's happened to him."

"I say it does mean just that!" Ellis rasped, his hand shooting across the bar and grabbing Sherman's shirt. The big man pulled Sherman toward him roughly, a neon beer sign lighting his heavily jowled face in a sinister way.

"Take it easy, John," Wilbur said. "We already jumped the gun once today."

"And look what happened," Ellis snarled, turning on him. "Old Pythias wanted to do everything by the book, and now he's gone." He shoved the bartender back into his glasses, and a few of them teetered and smashed on the floor. "I say we go up to that laboratory and either find Pythias Day or kill us a few Visitors for revenge. Now, what do you say?''

A murmur of approval rose from the men gathered in the bar. Sherman could see that they were turning into a mob at Ellis' instigation, but he could do nothing. He was afraid to speak out again after the way he'd been treated a moment ago.

"What are we waiting for?" Ellis bellowed. "Let's get going!"

The men tromped out of the bar, cradling their shotguns and rifles. Sherman had even seen a few handguns among them. It was as though the violence they had known when they fought the Visitors couldn't be contained. They had to go out and kill again. What would come of it, he couldn't say, but he'd been around long enough to know that it wouldn't be good.

Pythias couldn't run anymore. His body was so sore he was lucky to be moving at all, and he suffered from dozens of tiny cuts, welts, and bruises. Still, he pressed on through the dark forest, working his way inexorably back toward the village. Another few minutes and he'd be at the Backlick Road, the shortest way from Cutter's Cove to the cliffs. He wouldn't actually walk on the road, just stay near enough to see cars' headlights. Any sign of Visitors, he'd be back into the woods so deep even a pack of bloodhounds would never find him.

Moonlight occasionally pierced the tops of the birches and evergreens, providing just enough illumination to find his way.

Pythias broke off some dried twigs barring his way and stepped into a creekbed. It would be easier going if he followed this for a while, since it was bound to lead toward town.

A few minutes later, he caught the glimmer of headlights. Three, four, five vehicles, coming down the

Backlick Road. He could hear the drunken shouts of men.

Pythias stumbled forward out of the creekbed, running toward the cars in spite of the pain.

"Hey!" he shouted. "Over here!"

The cars kept moving, headlights forming cones of light that swayed from side to side as they screeched around curves. Pythias came out onto the road, screaming for them to stop. It was too late; the last car was a quarter of a mile ahead of him, and they would never see him in the dark.

"Goddamn drunks would probably have got me killed anyway," he said sourly, watching them drive up a cliffside at top speed.

Just as he was about to turn away, he spotted something on the ocean side of the cliff. It was a light, but not the moon. No, it was coming from the wrong direction. Something rose slowly over the top of the cliff.

"Good Lord. . . ." It was the skyfighter. The cars were driving right toward it now.

The skyfighter took a stationary position over the highest point of the cliff, where the road took a sharp turn. A bolt of blue light shot out of its bird-of-prey prow. The car in front caught fire, swerved, and went off the edge of the cliff. The screams of the men inside could be heard as they plummeted to their deaths.

A second car was hit, exploding right there in the road. The vehicle behind it tried to stop, the squeal of the brakes audible to Pythias. But it was no good. The driver couldn't stop in time. His car fishtailed into the burning wreckage, and both vehicles went over the cliff. The fourth car was picked off by a laser, roasting the men inside alive.

Pythias stood watching the carnage in horror, jaw agape. He waited for the last car to be destroyed. It was sufficiently far behind the others so that the driver was able to stop.

The men got out and started running back down the road—all but one of them.

One by one, the four fleeing men were vaporized by the laser fire. Only one remained alive now, looking up at the skyfighter with his long, straight blond hair streaming from under his hunter's cap.

Waiting for him to be killed, Pythias was amazed to see the skyfighter move away from the cliff, out over the ocean, and vanish without firing a single shot at the lone man.

Even from here, Pythias knew who he was.

The man was John Ellis.

Chapter 8

Jane Foley was worried. Her daughter had been missing since this afternoon. There was no answer at the lab, where Sarah worked for Dr. Brunk as his personal assistant. Worse, that brooding hulk John Ellis was telling everyone to stay indoors. And so, here she was, sitting in the kitchen drinking coffee while she should have been out looking for her daughter.

Sarah could take care of herself, of course. But if the Visitors were back, as Jane suspected . . . why didn't they go away and leave Earth in peace? If they'd asked for our help, I'm sure we would have given it to them, Jane thought.

She sipped her coffee and made a face. It was cold; she'd been sitting here at the table brooding so long the brew had turned to a bitter, icy liquid. Jane looked out the window at the streetlamps' glow in the dark. It looked very quiet out there. Surely it wouldn't hurt if she took a little drive along the coast to see if she could find out anything. She hadn't survived nearly sixty years by being a shrinking violet.

It only took a moment for her to get on a jacket and go out to the car. The streets were deserted, but it *was* eleven o'clock at night, after all. Two or three hours earlier, she had heard four or five cars full of shouting men drive past the house. They had cleared the way for her, no doubt, Jane thought sarcastically. As much noise as they were making, the Visitors would have heard them coming from miles away.

Jane started up the Honda Civic and backed out of the yard, the front-porch light guiding her way under the elms and maples. She headed off toward the north side of town, driving slowly and looking out for pedestrians. She lit a cigarette as soon as she got outside of town, making her way steadily toward Brunk Laboratories.

About ten minutes had passed when she saw a lone straggler. She immediately recognized the long gray beard and balding head. It was Pythias Day.

Jane pulled up on the shoulder across the road from where Pythias was walking, and rolled down the window.

"Need a lift, Mr. Day?" she called.

Pythias peered into her window. "Jane . . . Jane Foley, is that you?"

"Yes, 'tis. What are you doing out here?"

Pythias went around to the passenger's side and got into the Civic. Slamming the door shut, he said, "Jane, I don't know where to begin."

"Well, do you know anything about Sarah?"

He nodded. "She got away, with Dr. Brunk and the others up at the lab."

"Then the Visitors are up there?"

"Yes, they are."

"Do you know where Sarah and Dr. Brunk are?"

Pythias shook his head. "Can't say that I do, Jane. But I was there when the Visitors arrived, and everybody was gone from the laboratory buildings already."

"Thank God." This meant that Sarah was only hiding someplace. "Ever since Thaddeus died, that girl's all I've got."

"Ayuh." Pythias slumped down into the bucket seat, exhuasted.

"Pythias Day, you look a mess!" Jane exclaimed. "Let me take you home." She turned the car around.

"If you don't mind, Jane," said Pythias, "could I stay at your place a little while?"

"Why?" Jane glanced at him out of the corner of her eyes as she drove.

"It might prove dangerous for me to go home tonight."

Jane reacted with a double take, and the car swerved a little.

"There's somebody in this town who's a traitor," Pythias said, "and he's probably found out from his lizard masters that I know too much."

The front door of the tavern flew open, slamming against the wall. John Ellis stalked in and flung himself onto a stool. There were only a few lobstermen drinking at the bar and sitting in booths.

"Bourbon," Ellis gasped.

Sherman poured him a shot.

"Make it a double," John Ellis ordered.

"Okay." Sherman added another shot and handed him the glass. Ellis downed it in a single gulp. "They're all dead," he wheezed.

"Who?" Sherman asked, not wanting to believe what he knew he was about to hear.

"Everybody. Wilbur, Charlie, George, Hank, Dan—all of 'em, killed by Visitors."

"No." Sherman's eyes widened in terror.

"Yeah, blew our cars right off the road with laser fire. I don't think anybody got away except me."

The men who had been sitting in booths rose and gathered around Ellis. "Where'd it happen?" one of them asked.

"Up Blacklick Road, where it rises up the cliffside. It was the worst thing I've ever seen in my life."

"Somebody's gonna have to tell their wives," another man said.

"Maybe you could do it, Herb," Sherman said. "Go tell the preacher at least, and he can go around and see the women."

"Yeah." Herb backed away and went out the door to perform the disagreeable but necessary task.

John Ellis had another double bourbon and then asked, "Did Pythias Day show up yet?"

"Not yet."

Ellis nodded. "I wonder where he is," he said, his big red hand clutching his glass. "I wonder where he is."

Chapter 9

In the darkness of the storage closet, Willie contemplated the courage and integrity Pythias Day had shown, and was glad that he had freed the old human, in spite of the fact that he had taken Pythias' place.

His captivity had given Willie much time for meditation, and he could find no fault in the things he had done since he had come to Earth. He was right to side with the humans, even though it would probably now cost him his life. His people were wrong; it was their own inner turmoil that made them bring suffering on the primitive people of this world, not really the need for water or food. These were things that were available elsewhere in the galaxy. It seemed that his people had singled out the human race for punishment.

Willie's speculation was interrupted by the clicking of a key in the storage closet's lock, and light streamed into his makeshift cell, blinding him.

Without a word, a guard pulled him to his feet and led him into the laboratory proper. The long tables had been removed, and Ronald's troops were lined up along the walls of the narrow building's interior.

Willie was led between them, their crimson uniforms blazing in the morning light streaming through the windows. They all wore sunglasses, of course, so the light didn't bother them very much. Ronald was at their head, sitting in a director's chair on a low platform at the end of the gauntlet. Willie was pushed to his knees in front of Ronald.

"I have decided upon a punishment," the Visitor captain said, "which will be quite fitting, considering your love for this planet." Ronald's scales seemed to twitch with pleasure at the thought of what he had in store for Willie.

"You will be set free, Willie."

Willie lifted his head in surprise. What was Ronald talking about? Did he mean to convert Willie and send him among the resistance fighters as a spy? Surely he knew that wouldn't work. With his knowledge of the *preta-na-ma*, Willie could withstand the conversion process. No, he meant something else, but what?

"I have not yet determined the time and place for your liberation," Ronald said. "The setting will be most important. I must select it with the utmost care, for there you will die."

Willie raised his head again, and the guard pushed his face down onto the concrete floor.

"Take him away," Ronald commanded.

Willie was dragged back to the closet and locked up again in the dark. He understood that Ronald meant to torment him, and so he must return to his meditations, chanting from the ritual of Zon.

He began to chant, the knowledge that such singing was forbidden giving him strength.

When he got out of the bath, Pythias smelled coffee brewing in Jane's kitchen. He toweled himself dry, put on his rather unsavory clothes, and went downstairs to breakfast.

"Bacon and eggs," Jane said as he entered the kitchen.

"Smells grand." Pythias sat at the table while Jane served him. He thought about getting up to pour his own coffee, but Jane seemed to enjoy being his hostess.

When all the food was on the table, she sat down.

"So, Mr. Day," she said, buttering a piece of toast, "are you ready to tell me what's going on?"

"I hate to get you involved in this thing," he said.

"I'm already involved, so tell me."

Pythias set down his coffee cup. "The Visitors have found a collaborator in Cutter's Cove."

"You mentioned that last night. Who is it?"

"You might find this hard to believe, but it's John Ellis."

"John Ellis! That boy's lived here all his life! How could he do something like that?"

"I don't know. Maybe they brainwashed him, or maybe they promised him money or power. I don't know how they got him. All I know is that they got him." Pythias stared glumly at a framed print on the wall. "His father and mother must be turning over in their graves."

"But how can you be so sure?" Jane asked.

"There's no doubt about it. He led those men into a trap, making sure he was in the last car, which the Visitors didn't shoot at. The men got out and they were picked off, all but John. He stood right there and they never fired a shot anywhere near him."

"Does he know you saw him?"

"No."

"Then why are you worried about what he'll do?"

"Well, if he's in communication with the Visitors— and he must be—they've told him I've seen what's going on up at the lab. I think they'd like to keep what they're doing here quiet, to make it easier to find Dr. Brunk."

"That's who they're looking for, then—Dr. Brunk." The fact that her daughter was with Brunk made Jane uneasy. "Do you think they'll find him, Mr. Day?"

"I honestly don't know, Jane," Pythias said, spreading out his hands. "John Ellis has destroyed the local resistance in one fell swoop. If we can put together a new fighting force, we might be able to find him before the Visitors do. And, uh, Jane?"

"Yes, Mr. Day?"

"Please call me Pythias."

Chapter 10

"The way I see it," John Ellis said drunkenly, "they must have captured old Pythias and tortured the facts out of him. Once they knew how many of us there was, it was easy for 'em to figure out we'd be coming after the old buzzard. They just waited in that skyfighter until we came up the cliff road, and . . ."

"You think Pythias Day sold us out?" Herb Walsh asked, incredulous.

Ellis turned slowly toward him. "There wasn't anybody else had the chance, Herb. Pythias walked into a trap yesterday, the way I see it. Once they had him in their power, he had to break sooner or later."

"Pythias Day?" Herb persisted. "I can hardly believe he'd do something like that."

"You believe what you want," Ellis said, finishing his drink. "But all you have to do is put two and two together, and it adds up to our newly appointed sheriff setting us up last night."

"I still don't believe it," Herb said, but there was less conviction in his voice now.

"Why would Pythias do such a thing?" Mike Sherman asked. "I mean, those men were his friends and neighbors."

"I told you before—torture, or maybe he's just trying to get himself in good with the lizards in case they win. That way he'll be king of the hill around here once the shooting stops."

"But what if we beat the Visitors back, like we did

before?'' Sherman asked. ''That would mess up his plan, wouldn't it?''

''Not really. He'd come down off the mountain, claim he'd been a POW, and everybody'd call him a hero. I imagine old Pythias could live with that.''

The few men in Mike's Tavern murmured among themselves about the plausibility of John Ellis' scenario concerning Pythias Day's motivation for turning on his own people. The more Ellis talked about it, the more likely it seemed. And yet, none of them really wanted to believe Pythias would do such a thing.

''Damn it,'' Mike Sherman finally said, ''we're standing here in safety, condemning Pythias Day as a traitor, and for all we know those aliens have killed him.''

For once, John Ellis said nothing. How could he admit that he knew Pythias Day was alive? His best bet was to discredit the old coot before he showed up again. But where was he? He should have showed up by now, unless the Visitors were wrong. He might have been fatally wounded and died in the woods somewhere out of town. Or maybe he had slipped into town late last night or early this morning. He'd better check it out.

''I'll see you later,'' Ellis said, tossing some bills down on the bar.

The men grunted their farewells as he staggered out onto the wooden sidewalk in front of Mike's. He took a walk up Union and then crossed over onto State Street, where Day's house was.

Ten minutes later, he was standing in front of the whitewashed old two-story dwelling Day had shared with his late wife. As far as Ellis knew, the old codger had grown up in the same house. Family had been here for generations, so there wasn't much chance he'd have someplace else to go. And the place sure looked deserted. Still, there was only one way to find out if he was back.

Ellis walked boldly up to the front door and knocked. He waited a few moments and knocked again. Nobody answered. He tried one more time. When there was still no answer, he gave up, satisfied that there was nobody home.

Starting back toward Union Street, he began to believe for the first time that Pythias Day might be dead. He hadn't communicated with Ronald since last night, after all, and a lot could have happened since then. And then there was his earlier notion that Pythias Day might have died last night in the woods alone. It would serve the old meddler right, after what happened yesterday. That turncoat alien had been right in his hands, and Day had stopped him from stringing him up. Ronald wasn't very pleased about that, but at least they had that lizard resistance fighter where he couldn't do any harm now.

A car horn beeped, scaring him. He swung the barrel of his gun around, right at the startled face of Mrs. Foley, the widow, as she pulled into her driveway.

She shut off the engine and leaped out of the car. "Who do you think you're pointing that thing at, John Ellis?" she demanded.

"Sorry, Mrs. Foley," he apologized. "The way things have been going around here, I didn't know what it was, for a second there."

"That's because you're soused as usual, young man. And just what are you doing walking around here with a gun anyway?"

"Just trying to make sure everything's all right." He grinned.

Mrs. Foley looked skeptical. "Protecting little old me, are you, John?"

"Something like that."

"Well, don't bother. You're more likely to shoot me

than one of the Visitors, walking around here with a loaded gun and three sheets to the wind.''

"Hey, I'm sorry about pointing it at you. I was looking for Pythias Day.''

Her face darkened. Was that fear he saw there? "Why?"

"Well, he's been missing since yesterday," he said lamely.

"Don't you think he'd let it be known if he was back?" Mrs. Foley said.

"Yeah, I guess. . . .''

"Who put you up to this? Surely not the mayor. Mr. Day's the sheriff now that Mr. Evans is dead, you know. It's his job to worry about the safety of Cutter's Cove's citizens, not yours.''

"Yes, ma'am." He was getting tired of this old bat's lecturing. "Got to be going now, Mrs. Foley.''

"Good." She pulled a bag of groceries out of the Civic and slammed the door. There were two more bags in the car. Ellis was all the way to Union Street before he remembered that Sarah, the old woman's daughter, had disappeared with Dr. Brunk. That sure was a lot of groceries for one old woman.

Chapter 11

Jane locked the door and put the chain up before she put away the groceries. Pythias came softly down the stairs. "He was looking for me," he said.

"With a gun," Jane added. "I don't have a gun, or I'd give you one so you can protect yourself."

"I have a weapon," Pythias siad, stepping out of the shadows. He held the laser pistol that Willie had tossed to him as he made his escape from the occupied laboratory.

"Is that one of . . . their weapons?" Jane asked.

"Yeah, and a very accurate weapon it is too."

"You're not planning to use it on John Ellis, are you?"

"Not unless I have to," Pythias replied.

He went to the closet and got out his coat.

"Where are you going?" Jane asked.

"To my office," said Pythias, zipping up. He hid the laser under his jacket. "This foolishness has gone on just about long enough."

Jane didn't want him to go, but she sensed that it would do no good to plead with him.

"Be careful," she said.

He looked at her with affection. "Jane, I want to thank you for all you've done. I'm going to do my best to get your little girl back for you. Until then, keep a close watch out."

"I will." She closed the door behind him.

Pythias had a good twenty-minute walk to the courthouse, where the sheriff's office was located. Gone this morning were most of the aches and pains, the results of the alien cattle prod they'd used to torture him, as well as the minor burns, bruises, and cuts he'd sustained in his escape. Walking helped get the kinks out, and he felt better than he had any right to by the time he got to the office. This he attributed more to Jane Foley than anything else.

The first thing he should do was go tell the mayor what had happened last night. His honor could call out the local militia, or even get on the horn to the governor and see about getting out the National Guard.

He went into the glassed-in lobby of the courthouse/ city hall and walked toward the receptionist's desk.

"His honor in?" he asked, walking past the desk.

"Not yet, Sheriff."

Pythias stopped cold, smelling a rat. "He's not?" He glanced at his watch. "It's past ten o'clock. Where do you suppose he is?"

The woman, Peg MacGregor, looked concerned. "I don't know, Mr. Day. I called his house, but there's no answer."

Pythias nodded. He walked around the back, to the village motor pool, and got his patrol car. He'd only driven it once before, but it would get him there in spite of its ice cream lights on top and its buzzing radio plugged into the switchboard here in city hall.

Pythias ducked into his office, found the car keys hanging from a board, and went out to the patrol car.

Three minutes later he was pulling into the half-mile-long driveway belonging to the Cochrane estate. The mayor was the recipient of the largest fortune in these parts, his great-grandfather having made the family fortune in lumber in the nineteenth century. Ever since then, the Cochranes had been in public service.

It seemed unnaturaly still up here today, Pythias thought. There was usually a gardener raking leaves, or somebody painting one of the outbuildings, or somebody riding a horse across the spacious grounds. Not a soul stirred around the mansion.

Pythias got out of the car and walked up the mansion's front steps. He used the big brass knocker on the oak door, but no one answered.

"Funny," he said after trying again. There was a houseful of servants here, Mrs. Cochrane, and God only knew who else. Pythias tried to open the door, and it swung inward.

After a few seconds, he stepped gingerly inside. There was an empty foyer. The only sign that something might be wrong was a little mahogany table turned over on its side on the carpet.

The house was silent. Pythias moved quietly through its rooms. He found the first body in the kitchen—the cook, with a surprised look on her face and a hole burned in her breast. He found the maid on the stairs. Apparently she'd been trying to get away when she was cut down.

Mrs. Cochrane lay on the carpet in the upstairs hall. She was wearing a silk nightgown, her patrician face peering from between two banister spokes. She had been looking down at him all the time he had been prowling the downstairs, but of course she hadn't minded that he had entered uninvited.

Tom Cochrane was inside the master bedroom. He was on the floor only a couple paces from a huge canopied bed that must have been in this room for generations.

Unlike his wife, the mayor was lying faceup. He wore a puzzled look, as if he couldn't understand how such a thing could happen to him and his wife and their servants.

Pythias guessed that he'd find the gardener outside, and the handyman too, perhaps somewhere among the hedges or in one of the sheds or other outbuildings. He shook his head.

They might have come here looking for him—him or Randall Brunk. Had John Ellis told the Visitors he suspected their enemies had been hiding here, or had the mayor and his family been killed just to demoralize the town of Cutter's Cove?

He sighed, thinking that he would probably never know.

Chapter 12

Willie was being fed so that he would have his strength when Ronald set him free. Ronald wanted Willie to provide good sport when he hunted him down. Rejecting the rodents that were brought to him, Willie devoured only vegetables. Since he had worked with the resistance, he had devoted himself to the *preta-na-ma*, in which the eating of flesh was forbidden. He found that vegetarianism gave him stamina that he had never possessed before, even back on the home world, when he was little more than an eggling.

Willie had been raised in the provinces, where people still believed in the old religion. They would never succeed in eradicating the *preta-na-ma* in the Sirian system. The more they suppressed it, the stronger its adherents became.

How had his world come to such a sorry state? It seemed to him that his people were essentially good, and yet they had somehow permitted this evil form of government to dominate them until they all lived in fear.

The humans claimed that their world had known such governments, but never on a global scale, and they had barely dreamed of totalitarianism on an interplanetary scale, much less the interstellar terror they suffered now.

Like all those who had been sent to Earth, Willie had been indoctrinated thoroughly. He had been taught that the humans were inferior beings, incapable of pure reason without emotion.

To prove that the Sirians had a right to conquer Earth,

the instructors cited the age of dinosaurs as evidence that reptilian life had dominated the planet long before humankind. The inability of the human race to form a worldwide government to arbitrate their regional differences was mentioned as further proof. It was the right— no, the duty—of Willie's people to civilize these beasts.

Willie had almost believed it, until he had come to Earth and seen what they were really like, these humans. He had been loved by them, and he found their despised emotion as not such a bad thing. A human woman had loved him, and she had died because of her love. How could he turn his back on that?

He must endeavor to escape from this place. Otherwise, Ronald would kill him like a wild beast. Perhaps he could overpower the guard when he brought food. No, they would never allow themselves to be fooled twice in the same way. In spite of the obvious limitations of the military mind, Ronald was not stupid.

Willie would simply have to wait and take his chances. If Ronald gave him any chance at all, it was better than the chance he had here, rotting in this filthy closet.

That was it, then. He would wait and do everything Ronald wanted him to do. He would not permit Ronald to torment him; instead, he would put his faith in the power of the *preta-na-ma*. This, Ronald would never understand.

Willie began to chant the ritual of Zon, to give himself strength and to weaken his enemies.

His voice echoed in the tiny enclosure, a pleasurable sound . . . at least to Willie.

Outside the little storage room, the guards cringed at the sound of the renewed chanting from within. When their master approached, the two of them were relieved by the interruption.

"He still sings?" Ronald asked in amazement. "Does he think this is a festive occasion?"

"I don't know, sir," one of the guards said.

Ronald waved him to silence. "I didn't expect you to answer, you fool."

Ronald stared at the locked door. After a long moment, he slammed his bunched claw against it. The singing stopped for a short time and then resumed.

Ronald pounded on the door again. "Silence!" he shouted.

The singing stopped again. "As you wish," Willie said from the other side of the door.

Somehow this did not placate Ronald. "If he begins that horrible chanting again," he said menacingly, "call for me at once. He breaks the law every time he chants from the ritual of Zon."

The guards cowered at the very name of Zon, the forbidden faith.

Ronald stalked away, walking the length of the building and going outside. He went to the skyfighter and uttered a subvocal command that sent the ramp down and opened the hatch.

He entered the ship and made certain that the hatch was closed behind him. He then uttered another command, and a panel, seven feet by three, emerged from the wall.

Removing his uniform, cap, and glasses, Ronald opened the panel, which was shaped like an Egyptian sarcophagus. He lay inside, and the panel closed over him.

A moment later, a vibration shook the tiny cubicle. A warm chemical bath washed over Ronald's squamous flesh, and tendrillike filaments worked on the fluid covering him as it cooled and hardened into a substance indistinguishable from human flesh.

When he emerged, Ronald was the image of a naked

human male, save for his yellow, reptilian eyes. He opened a box with a selection of plastic eyes and picked a pair of green ones. He inserted them in his pseudo-skin human face, and then examined himself in a mirror. Once a wig was in place, no one would know he wasn't human.

The perfect disguise to wear on a mission to Cutter's Cove.

Chapter 13

As Pythias cruised the streets of Cutter's Cove and the outlying regions, he notice that people tended to shun him. You would have thought he was a Visitor himself, he thought, coming back into town on the Backlick Road.

"That's it!" he shouted. It was Ellis, claiming he was working with the Visitors, distracting people from realizing the truth. Well, maybe it was time to pay John Ellis a little visit. Pythias had a pretty good idea of where to find that no-good son of a bitch.

He turned up Union Street and parked in front of Mike's Tavern. Making sure the laser was hidden under his coat, he stepped up onto the wooden sidewalk and opened the barroom door.

Ellis, sitting at the bar, did not look up.

"Hello, John," Pythias said.

Ellis raised his fair, surly head, and his jaw dropped as he saw who it was.

"Well, I'll be damned," Mike Sherman said. "What are you doing here, Pythias? Everybody thought you were dead or captured by them lizards."

"I was captured, all right."

"Then the lizard led you into a trap?" Herb Walsh asked.

"That was what I thought at first," Pythias said, moving to the other end of the bar, away from John Ellis. "Beer, Mike."

"That wasn't what happened?" Mike said as he drew the beer from the tap.

"No, it wasn't."

"Well, what did happen?" demanded Herb. "I never knew a man could stretch out a story like you, Pythias."

Pythias smiled. "He helped me escape."

"What?" they all cried.

As the men buzzed about what Pythias had just said, John Ellis rose off his bar stool and lumbered ominously toward the older man.

"What the hell are you talking about, Day?" he shouted.

"You heard me, John." Pythias took a long sip of beer and smacked his lips.

"Everybody knows the Visitors don't just let you go after they've captured you."

"Didn't claim they did," Pythias said, running his fingers along the side of the glass, rubbing off the moisture. "The Visitors captured Willie and me. Since he was one of them, they didn't realize he was a member of the resistance, like he told us."

John Ellis snarled.

"But he was." Pythias looked at him sharply. "I know it, because the first chance he got, he came and helped me get away from the room they had me locked in."

"No kidding," Mike Sherman said.

"No, sir," Pythias replied, taking another sip of his beer. "No kidding at all."

"I never heard such a crock of shit in my entire life," John Ellis said.

"Is that right, John?" Pythias said, drawing himself up to his full height as he stood. "You got a better story?"

Ellis lost his imposing anger; he began to look confused. "What do you mean?"

"You seem awful sure what I'm saying isn't true. What's your version?"

"Why, I wasn't there. I . . ."

"But you took some men out last night, didn't you? To find me, you claimed. Isn't that right?"

"Yeah, that's right, but what—"

"That's what I want to know, John," Pythias said, looking straight into Ellis' evasive eyes. "How come you're the only one who came back?"

"I . . . was lucky," Ellis said as his tiny red-rimmed eyes darted from one side of the room to the other.

Everyone was staring at him now, wondering the same thing Pythias wondered. Why had twenty-five men gone out, and only John Ellis come back?

"You can't prove nothing." Ellis turned toward the bar, where his gun was leaning.

"I wouldn't if I were you, John," Pythias said coolly. "These things burn like hell."

Ellis turned around and saw the laser pistol in Pythias' hand.

"I'm taking you down to the station for questioning," said Pythias. "And I might arrest you for the murders of those men."

"You out of you mind, Day?" Ellis bellowed. "You haven't got a shred of evidence."

"We'll see about that, boy."

Ellis glanced at his shotgun, wondering if he could make it over to it without getting hit.

"Don't even think about going for that peashooter, son," Pythias said. "Or I'll burn you down to a cinder right where you stand."

Ellis put up his hands, feeling sweat run down his face.

"Now, march," Pythias instructed.

Ellis marched.

Chapter 14

Jane was doing the laundry. She lifted a box of detergent, racking her brain for the ten thousandth time, trying to think of where Sarah and Dr. Brunk could possibly be hiding. She stared mutely at the box of Tide, and then the image of an ocean wave washed through her mind.

"The ocean," she said aloud. "Dr. Brunk's got a cabin on some island out in the ocean."

She set down the box and went to the phone to call Pythias Day. But then she thought of what John Ellis had done last night. There was no telling who else might be involved with the Visitors, and there were ways to listen in on the phone conversations. It would be better if she went down to city hall herself.

She rushed to the closet and put on her jacket, and then hurried out to the car. Realizing she had forgotten her purse when she went to lock the door, she ran back inside and picked it up.

A few seconds later she was in the Civic, revving up the engine and backing out onto the street. A pickup truck roared by, honking at her. She slammed on the brakes and waited for him to pass and then started out of the yard a little more slowly.

A big man, wearing a blue business suit, entered the tiny sheriff's office in the back of city hall, the bell ringing over his head.

He looked at the bell oddly for a moment and then

down at Pythias; the latter seemed to detect a familiar look in the stranger's green eyes.

"What can I do for you, mister?" Pythias asked.

"I understand you have my cousin incarcerated here," the man said.

"What's his name?" Pythias asked, thinking there must be some mistake.

"John Ellis."

"Yeah, we got him locked up back there, all right." Pythias opened a desk drawer to get the keys out. "I never knew he had a cousin around here."

"You're quite right, Sheriff," the man said, smiling. I'm Bill Ellis, from Bangor. I haven't seen John in years, but I was in Rockland on business and I decided to stop over here and visit him, since it's so close."

"He's only been here a short time," Pythias said. "How does it happen you've found out about it already."

"Well, I went to the nearest bar, and they said he was here." Bill Ellis looked troubled. "I hope it's nothing very serious."

"Just questioning, for now." Pythias led him back into the cell block. John Ellis sat sulking in the cell, the effect of the liquor he had drunk weighing heavily upon him now.

"John," Pythias said, "there's someone here to see you."

John Ellis looked up, and his sullen expression changed. But it wasn't the look Pythias expected. He looked puzzled.

"Of course you don't recognize me," Bill Ellis said. "You haven't seen me since you were eight. I was stationed in the Middle East for years. I'm your cousin Bill . . . from Bangor."

"Oh, Bill. . . ." Ellis sat up. "What are you doing here?"

"Just coincidence. I was in Rockland and thought I'd

stop over in Cutter's Cove to see my long-lost cousin. What a surprise."

"For both of us." There was merriment in Ellis' eyes now. "What a day you picked to find me."

Pythias left them alone, reasonably satisfied that it was in fact only a coincidence Bill Ellis had come today of all days. Stranger things had happened, he supposed.

Nevertheless, he pulled his chair up where he could see the two men talking, Bill Ellis leaning against the bars as they chatted. Bill looked like a man of means, unfortunately. He would probably let John talk him into bailing him out.

No sense in speculating about it, Pythias decided. Whatever happened now, he knew the truth about John Ellis. And John Ellis couldn't be certain how much he knew either. As long as he was in jail, Ellis couldn't communicate with the Visitors, and as soon as he got out, Pythias would keep him under surveillance.

Pythias sighed, thinking how nice it would be if he could get a deputy. There was a shortage of men in the village these days, though. Only the drunks at Mike's were left, and Pythias didn't want another weakling like John Ellis, who might shoot him in the back to get in good with the Visitors. No, he would have to go it alone. He had been selfish to involve Jane Foley in this thing. He should have taken a ride home and left it at that. And yet, he was glad he had stayed at her house the night before. She had needed comfort as much as he did, and so it wasn't a bad thing that he'd done.

At that moment, a familiar blue Honda Civic pulled up into the parking lot. Jane Foley jumped out and ran toward the office like a girl, her skirt flying behind her.

She burst into the office excitedly, slamming the door, the bell jangling overhead.

"Pythias!" she cried. "I think I know where Sarah

and Dr. Brunk are. Brunk owns an island a little way off the coast!''

Pythias tried to shush her, but it was too late. He glanced into the cell block and saw Bill and John Ellis both staring attentively at Jane.

Chapter 15

Sarah Foley put a blanket over Dr. Brunk as he slept. He had a history of heart trouble, she knew, and she wouldn't permit him to do anything very strenuous, though he often complained vociferously about her pandering. It was hard to convince him that the strain on his heart from recent events was enough, perhaps too much. He had to be careful, what with the human race dependent on his survival.

Closing the cabin door softly behind her, Sarah went for a walk. Long twilight shadows fell across the pine-needle bed around the cabin. The days were getting shorter now that fall was coming in. There was a chill in the air that hadn't been noticeable a week ago. Well, chopping firewood would give her something to do in the days to come, she thought.

Entering the shadowy forest, she thought about the events of recent days. As the Visitors had moved into rural areas, they had come to Cutter's Cove in a small group, apparently thinking they could easily terrorize such a provincial outpost. They had been surprised at the anger with which the local citizenry responded. A number of skirmishes had broken out, one of them right on Union Street.

The Visitors had killed the sheriff, but they lost a number of soldiers themselves. One of those was only wounded, and he had been taken to Brunk Labs, where Dr. Brunk was working on a new toxin. He used the alien as a guinea pig, extracting a virus from him that he then recombined with new genetic material. The virus he came up with was almost impossible to fight, hiding in the aliens' nerve endings while dormant and lethal when active. At least that was what was hypothesized. Unfortunately, the alien died of wounds substained in the fight, and Dr. Brunk was never able to test it on him.

The resistance was to send a friendly Visitor who would voluntarily take his place, but the day he was to arrive they had received word that the aliens knew about what was going on at Brunk Labs, and they had been forced to desert the compound.

Sarah followed the markings on trees that Dr. Brunk had pointed out to her. The woods were so thick that nobody would ever guess people were living here. Even if someone came to the island, they might explore it without ever finding the cabin. It was almost invisible, unless you knew where it was. Designed for solitude, it provided them with the perfect hiding place while the Visitors searched for them.

A hare leaped across her path, startling her a little.

"That's no lizard," she said aloud. And yet there was a lot of wildlife on the few square miles of this island. Dr. Brunk had told her there were bears and that they should always bolt the door at night when the big beasts came rummaging about looking for food. Sarah wondered how the bears had ever got out here. She imagined them as symbols of the tenacity of life. Had a pregnant female bear swum out here long ago in search of a blueberry patch, and then decided it was too nice a spot to leave?

She assumed that if she didn't bother the bears, they wouldn't bother her. Maybe she would even put out food for them, if they were here for a few days.

But the didn't know how long they were going to be here, of course. They had no way of telling how things were going on the mainland. Perhaps the Visitors had been repulsed again. And then again, perhaps not.

Sooner or later, they would have to go back to the mainland. They had brought virtually nothing out to the island with them, just a few things that had been lying around in the laboratory, including some bread and cold cuts out of the refrigerator in the lounge. Such a small amount of food wouldn't last very long. There were some fishing rods and tackle in the cabin, of course, and they could always share the blueberries with the bears.

Sarah hoped it wouldn't come to that. The resistance would surely make it safe for them to go back to the mainland soon.

She tried not to think of the alternative as she walked. In a while she came to the shore, the salt air invigorating as she looked at the choppy waves.

The boat was down a little farther, well hidden between two big rocks. Gulls cawed over the mainland in the distance, over a mile away. Here and there, heavily wooded islands projected like green beards out of the glittering sea. She wondered how many of them had cabins on them. Most likely nobody would be on them this late in the year, even if there were cabins.

The water lapping the big glacial rocks made a soft, susurrant sound, soothing and beautiful.

Suddenly she caught a glimpse of something on the horizon. Before she could tell what it was for certain, it disappeared behind an island.

Something that big and reflecting the dying sunlight that way could only be a ship. But no ship would be this close to the shore, unless it was a very large yacht. But something told her it wasn't as innocent as that.

The thing emerged, not beside the island, but *over* it. It hummed with a power never heard of on this world. It was a Visitor craft—a skyfighter.

Sarah backed away from the water's edge and headed

toward the woods before it could spot her. She ran through the woods, falling once over a gnarled root, to warn Dr. Brunk that the Visitors were coming to get them.

Chapter 16

"I'm so sorry, Pythias," Jane said, standing in the front doorway of the Day home. "How can a woman live almost sixty years and never learn not to shoot off her mouth?"

"Stop criticizing yourself, and come in," Pythias said. He led her into the living room. "I was just about to have a cup of coffee. Would that suit you?"

"Thank you." She sat down after Pythias took her coat.

Pythias disappeared for a moment and returned bearing two mugs filled with steaming coffee. He set one down on an end table next to the couch where Jane was sitting, and held the other as he joined her.

"You couldn't know I had arrested John Ellis," Pythias said. "And even if you had known it, you couldn't possibly have predicted that his cousin would show up today and bail him out."

"What a coincidence," Jane said dryly.

"That's what I've been thinking too." Pythias sipped his coffee. "Heck of a coincidence—and I could swear I've met Bill Ellis before, even though he says he's never laid eyes on me in his whole life."

"I don't see that it makes much difference," Jane said. "What's important is that he bailed John out."

"Cold, hard cash. Something I couldn't have foreseen when I arrested him. I suppose I could arrest him again— drunk and disorderly, carrying a concealed weapon, something like that. But he'll just call his cousin if I do

and be back out on the street again before you could spit
on the sidewalk.''

"Which I have no intention of doing, Pythias.''

He favored her with one of his rare smiles. ''Call me
Pyth.''

"Pyth? I never heard anybody call you that.'' She
nearly laughed.

"My Jeannie used to.''

Jane nodded, understanding that this was quite a
compliment he was paying her. He was putting her on the
same exalted plane as his late wife. Her first impulse had
been to laugh, but now she was touched. As far as she
knew, Pythias had taken up with no other woman since
Jeannie Day's death seven years ago.

She was deeply moved.

"The question is," Pythias said, as though nothing
had passed between them, "where do we go from here?''

He didn't seem to notice her wiping away a tear with
the back of her hand. "Well," she replied, "where *do* we
go from here—Pyth?''

"I thought you'd never ask.'' He smiled again,
showing strong white teeth amid the shaggy beard. "We
go out to that island before the Visitors do. After all, they
don't know which island it is, and there's a lot of them
around Cutter's Cove.''

"Good idea, except that I don't know which island it is
either.''

This stopped him cold. "You don't?''

"No, I only remember that Sarah once told me Dr.
Brunk owned a little island off the coast. A place where
he goes to relax and fish in the summertime.''

Pythias' brow furrowed in deep thought. "Somebody
around here must know where it is.''

"I don't think so," said Jane. "He's a very private
man.''

"Well, we've got to find it, one way or another.''

Pythias set down his coffee cup. "I've got some maps here that show the islands along the coast, along with the inlets and bays. Maybe we can at least figure out where to start by taking a look at 'em."

"Maybe," Jane said, trying to sound hopeful.

"If we could get a helicopter or a plane," Pythias mused, "we could fly low over those islands and spot 'em, but since the Visitors have been skulking around here, all the public safety departments are shorthanded, so it's not likely we can do something like that on short notice."

"What, then?"

"We'll have to go by sea."

"Pyth, that might take too long."

He looked at her with genuine regret. "Jane, I don't know what else we can do."

He went to a glassed-in cabinet and pulled out a number of scroll-like, rolled-up maps.

"Remember," he said as he smoothed them out, "the Visitors don't know this area as well as we do, and they don't know which island they're on either."

"But they do have those skyfighter things, so they can spot them from the air." Jane was chilled, thinking of what they might do to her little girl. "Oh, God."

Pythias put down the map he was looking at and turned to Jane. "Come on now, Jane. Buck up. We can't have you falling apart now."

Tears began welling up under her eyelids and spilling onto her cheeks. "I thought when we sent her to college, she'd be able to get a good job, and I was so happy when she ended up as Dr. Brunk's assistant right near home. I never thought it would put her life in danger."

Pythias didn't know what to say as she stood there crying in his living room. Instead of speaking, he went to her and held her until her tears stopped.

Chapter 17

John Ellis had been driving his old Ford Pinto along Route 31, inland toward the state's interior, for a few miles. He was accompanied by his "cousin," Bill Ellis.

"You turn east at the next intersection," Bill Ellis said.

"You want to go back to the coast?"

"By a circuitous route," Bill explained. "We'll come in from the north and take the cliff road to Brunk Laboratories."

"Who are you?" Ellis asked suspiciously. It occured to him that his savior might be working for Pythias Day. They could be trying to find out what he knew about the Visitors.

"Don't you know me, Johnny?" Bill rasped. "I'm your faithful old cousin Bill."

"I don't have a cousin named Bill," John Ellis said. He slowed to turn on a dirt road he knew from hunting trips. "This road will take us back to the ocean eventually."

"Excellent."

"I'll drop you where you want to go, man, and I thank you kindly for getting me out of jail."

"You'll do more than thank me, John Ellis."

There was something in the guy's tone that chilled Ellis. "Who are you?" he repeated.

As he drove down the lonely dirt road, Ellis tried to keep an eye on his savior.

"Don't you know who I am?"

"No."

A bizarre hissing sound escaped Bill's lips, and he lifted one hand to his face.

"What are you doing?"

Bill tore at the flesh on his left cheek. His nails dug in so sharply that John expected blood to spurt all over the dash.

Something else happened.

Bill pulled a piece of flesh out until it snapped off. The entire left side of his face came away, revealing a shiny dark green carapace beneath.

"Did you think I was sent by the ACLU?" Bill asked, laughing hideously.

He popped his thumb into his left eye socket. The eyeball came free, falling into his other hand. There was no optic nerve, no ganglia, no blood, just a plastic sphere lying in Bill's hand.

"It's a sensory scanner," Bill said. "A neat little device, don't you think?"

It was all John could do to keep the car on the road, much less hold a conversation about the eyeball. He was really scared, his hands shaking so badly he was having trouble steering.

"Now do you know who I am?" the creature sitting in the passenger's seat of John Ellis' car said.

"Ronald," Ellis said. "You're Ronald. I should have known."

"You should have, indeed," Ronald said, tearing off the rest of his pseudo-skin face.

Ellis always got a little nervous when he was this close to the alien captain. The had always met at a rendezvous point deep in the woods, where no one was likely to chance upon them. But Ronald had not shocked him as he did now.

"I am not through with you, John Ellis," Ronald said. "Not yet."

"That's all right with me," Ellis said, regaining his composure a little. "You know I'm on your side."

"You have done well, leading your men to the slaughter night before last, just as you were instructed. It more than made up for your bungled attempt at executing the traitor Willie."

"I did what I could," Ellis said humbly.

"Yes, and you will receive your due," rasped Ronald, "when the time comes."

"I can wait a little longer. I've been waiting all my life, growing up in that shack on the outskirts of Cutter's Cove, my old man a drunk. I've been alone since I was sixteen, when he kicked off. I never knew my mother, never had a pot to piss in. But things are gonna be different when you take over around here, aren't they, Ronald?"

"Yes," the alien hissed. "Things will be different."

Ellis kept driving, the road so narrow pine needles sometimes slapped against the windshield as the Pinto collided with low branches. He didn't like dealing with lizards, but once they'd completed their conquest of Earth, he'd be in charge around here. And all those people who'd turned up their noses at him all his life would be taking orders from him.

"Slow this vehicle," Ronald said. "I must put my pseudo skin back on in case someone sees us."

"Nobody's gonna see you," Ellis told him. "When we come out of the woods, we'll be close by the cliff road."

"Excellent."

"When are you going to send out a patrol to look for Brunk on the islands?"

"I have already communicated a command to that effect," Ronald said.

"So you'll have Brunk soon—and the girl." Ellis thought about Sarah Foley's soft beauty. He had wanted her ever since he was in his teens, but she'd always been unattainable, like a goddess.

Maybe Ronald would give her to him.

Chapter 18

Jake Futterman and Charlie Fitzgerald had come all the way from Manhattan to do some hunting. They had driven for hundreds of miles, rifles in the trunk of Charlie's Cadillac, and now they were stuck in some little one-horse town on the coast of Maine.

"Do you really think we had to come this far to find good hunting?" Jake asked sarcastically. "We can't hunt out in the ocean, you know."

"Look." Charlie gestured out the window at the virgin forests bordering the little town. "There's bound to be good hunting around here. All we need to do is find some local boy to guide us."

"Yeah, right. I should have gone to the Poconos with Ethel."

"Come on, Jake. We'll get us a room, buy a bottle of bourbon. Who knows, maybe we'll even get a little hunting in."

Jake sighed.

"Look, right over here—Pine Tree Motor Lodge. What did I tell you?"

Charlie pulled over at the motor lodge. Safely in the parking lot, he cut the engine and opened the car door to get out.

"What if they don't have any vacancies?" Jake said.

"Are you kidding?" Charlie gesticulated with his left hand as his right held the door open. "I'm working with this guy, what? twelve years now, and he still asks me questions like this. Jake, we came up here to have a good time. It's gonna be all right."

Jake muttered something incomprehensible as he got out. Together, they walked toward the office of the Pine Tree Motor Lodge, wearing their bright orange Day-Glo hunting jackets and caps.

Inside, they were confronted with a surly Down Easterner watching wrestling on an ancient black-and-white television.

"Can we get a room?" Charlie asked.

"Why not?" the hayseed asked rhetorically. "Got plenty of 'em."

They signed in and paid the man, and Charlie asked him where they might find a guide for hire.

"Try the tavern up on Union Street," the wrestling fan instructed them. "Up the hill and turn right. Can't miss it."

"Right. Thank you." Jake and Charlie went out to get their things out of the car, since it was obvious there was no bellboy available. Once they'd put the rifles and luggage in their room—which featured a horse-head lampshade—they set out to find the tavern.

"He didn't even tell us the name of the place," Jake complained.

"How many drinking establishments you think a hamlet like this has, Jake?" Charlie asked, wheeling the Caddy around the corner. "You know, you worry too much. When the Visitors came, you thought it was the end of life on Earth as we know it. You said the human race couldn't fight against such an advanced race. But then it turned out that some scientists developed a toxin that makes it impossible for the Visitors to live in a below-freezing climate."

"There are still some of them around."

"Only until the first frost, pal."

"They'll find a cure for it."

"Then we'll develop something else. You know how science is."

"Maybe," Jake muttered.

"There it is," Charlie said, spying Mike's Tavern.

He pulled up in front, and they got out of the car and hopped up onto the wooden sidewalk.

"Just like in a western," Jake observed.

"I knew you'd like it here," Charlie said, opening the tavern door.

It was dark inside, where a few old men sat with their drinks in silence. Jake and Charlie stood on the threshold for a moment and then entered.

"What can I get you, gents?" the bartender asked, eyeing their hunters' togs.

"Beer," Charlie said. "Two beers."

"Coming right up."

After they were served, Charlie said, "We hear there's good hunting around here."

"Sometimes," the bartender replied.

"Well, since we don't know our way around here, we want to hire a guide."

"Not too many ablebodied men left around town," the barkeep said. "Those who are still around are in what's left of the militia. Might be some action with the Visitors coming up soon."

"Yeah, we know about that in New York," Jake said.

"Well, they're moving out into the country now."

"Hope you have better luck than we did," Jake said.

Charlie shot him a disapproving glance. "We didn't come here to discuss politics," he said. "We came to do a little hunting. One of you gents guide us?"

"I'll guide you." A burly blond man slid out of the booth all the way in the back of the tavern.

"All right," said Charlie.

Arrangements were made, and a few mintues later Jake and Charlie left Mike's Tavern with John Ellis.

Chapter 19

Pythias spent a good part of the day in the hall of records trying to find something about an island owned by the Brunk family. There were seventy-odd islands, all within a short distance of Cutter's Cove, but there was no deed under that name.

Pythias decided that he must have been looking under the wrong name. Perhaps the island had belonged to Brunk's mother's family, or perhaps the family of his ex-wife. It was impossible to tell. There had to be some record, but how to find it? He realized the difference between a trained lawman and a dedicated amateur like himself. Sheriff Evans probably had been through this sort of thing before and would have known exactly what to do.

He closed the heavy black binder through which he had been fruitlessly poring, and stood up, placing his palm on the aching small of his back. He picked up the binder and returned it to Mrs. Snodgrass at the desk.

"Any luck?" the elderly woman asked, accepting the binder.

"No, not yet."

"That's funny," said Mrs. Snodgrass.

"Oh?" Pythias arched an eyebrow. "Why's that?"

"Well, Dr. Brunk's not from around here, so you'd think any real estate transaction would have been noticed, what with Cutter's Cover being such a small town and all."

"He must have wanted to avoid that," Pythias mused. "Keep it a secret."

"But why would he do that?"

"Maintain his privacy, I guess." Pythias noticed a sly look on the old lady's face. "You get any ideas why he might do that, Mrs. Snodgrass?"

"To avoid paying a high price."

"I don't understand," Pythias said.

"Well, he'd been around here long enough to know that there's often one price for local people and another for city slickers like him. And he's smart enough fellow to figure out how to get around that problem."

Pythias nodded. "I see what you're driving at."

"I thought you would." Mrs. Snodgrass smiled.

"But that still doesn't tell us who his intermediary was, if your hypothesis is correct."

"No, I can't help you there but I can ask around."

"Thanks. I'll do the same, and maybe between the two of us we can come up with something."

Pythias left the hall of records and went around the side of the building to his office. One thing about a small town, he mused, you don't have to go far to find what you need—if you can find it at all, that is.

He was surprised to find Herb Walsh waiting for him. Herb was standing in front of the office, shifting his weight from one foot to the other, looking very uneasy.

"What can I do for you, Herb?" Pythias asked. "Bar close down?"

Herb glanced down at his feet. "Maybe I deserve that," he said. "Drinking away all my time while all this bad business is going on."

"I'm sorry I said that," Pythias told him. "Come on in, Herb."

They went inside, and Pythias indicated a chair by his desk. The younger man sat down as Pythias made coffee. "You got something to tell me, Herb?"

"It might not be important."

"Can't hurt to tell me what it is then, can it?"

"I guess not."

Pythias left the coffee to brew and sat down at his desk. "This ought to make it seem a little more official," he said. "Of course, I haven't got one of those little doodads with my name on it yet, but I'm doing what I can to remedy that situation."

Herb smiled a little at that. "Mr. Day, I was really surprised to hear you're the new sheriff. You just don't seem like that type, if you don't mind my saying so."

"The late mayor couldn't get anybody else," Pythias said. "Now, son, what is it you came to tell me?"

"It's about John Ellis."

Pythias leaned forward to hear Herb's hoarse voice. "What about him?"

"Couple of things. First, he's been telling everybody that you must be working with the Visitors, since you got that laser pistol."

Pythias shrugged.

"I kind of doubt it," Herb said. "You see, I've known John all my life, and he doesn't have any cousins in Bangor or anywhere else. His father was all he had, and now that the old man's gone he's said a thousand times he's the last living member of his family and glad of it."

"Jesus Christ!" Pythias shouted. "I knew there was something phony about that guy."

"That's not all," Herb added. "John volunteered as a guide for two would-be hunters from New York today."

Pythias was puzzled. "So?"

"Well, it might be he just wants to pick up some extra money, but I never knew John to guide hunters before. He always kind of acted like it was beneath him."

Pythias nodded. "Thanks, Herb."

"What I told you won't go past this office, will it?"

"Not unless we need you to testify in court."

"I'll do what I have to," Herb said.

Pythias shook his hand. "I'm glad you came in to tell me all this."

Herb nodded and rose.

"Coffee's about ready."

"No, thanks," Herb said. "I better get back."

Chapter 20

John Ellis was conspicuously absent from the funeral. The mayor and his wife were buried in the little cemetery behind the Methodist Church at nine o'clock in the morning. It was a short service, Reverend Fisher reading from the Psalms in the crisp autumn air.

Pythias wasn't really surprised that John couldn't make it, since he was probably at least partly responsible for these murders.

Standing beside Pythias, Jane Foley stifled a tear as the mayor and Mrs. Cochrane were lowered into the ground. Try as she might, she couldn't help thinking that this might be the same fate that had befallen Sarah, her only child.

When the last words were spoken, the mourners—including most of the citizens of Cutter's Cove—filed along a narrow path down the hill toward the brick church. The gilt of the leaves was brilliant in the bright sunlight, and the sound of children playing in the schoolyard nearby could be heard over the soft voices of the dispersing funeral party.

"I'm not having much luck," Pythias said, clearly discouraged. "If I could just find out who bought that land as a dummy for Randall Brunk."

"Somebody around town must know," Jane offered, glad to have something to take her mind off her missing daughter, if only for a second.

"And then there's also the problem of John Ellis and those hunters."

"I should think you'd be grateful for that. At least John will be out of your hair for a while."

Pythias looked out at the ocean. The gleaming waves broke around island after island, as far as the eye could see.

"Might be quicker if I just took out a boat and searched those islands myself."

"Pyth!" Jane cried. "Look!"

In the distance, something that looked like a white bird of prey skimmed over the surface of the ocean, occasionally rising to hover over one of the islands.

"I can't waste any more time," Pythias said. "I've got to start looking right away."

They walked to the car quickly and got in.

"I'll take you home," Pythias said.

"No, Pyth, I want to go with you."

"Might be dangerous to the health."

Jane smirked. "Staying alone by myself might be dangerous too—to my mental health."

"You know something, Jane," Pythias said.

She looked at him, expecting an argument. "What?"

"You're a hell of a woman."

She smiled at him. "Does that mean you don't mind if I come along?"

"Of course I don't mind."

They drove down to the old ocean road, pulling up to Don Curtis' shack. Don, a veteran of fifty years of setting lobster traps, came out to greet them.

"What can I do you for, Sheriff?" he said, corncob pipe clenched between his yellow teeth. "How are you, ma'am?"

"Need to charter a boat, Don."

"Got plenty of boats. Looks like you've come to the right place."

"We need something that will move fairly fast," Pythias explained. "Got a lot of territory to cover."

They walked out onto the pier to look over Don's boats, settling on a small craft with an outboard Evinrude engine.

"That'll get the job done," Don said, quoting them a rental fee. " . . . unless of course it's official business, Sheriff." He spit casually in the direction of the cannery.

Pythias thanked him, grateful that there were still a few like Don Curtis left in Cutter's Cove. He and Jane clambered into the little boat with Curtis's assistance. After a few abortive jerks, Pythias managed to get the motor roaring. He pointed the prow over the breakers toward the nearest of the myriad islands in and around the harbor.

"We could be out here quite a while," he shouted.

"Maybe we should have brought something to eat," Jane replied.

"We'll have to go in to shore when we run out of gas anyway. Unless we're really lucky, this could take a long time, Jane."

Islands rose from the ocean like the caps of huge mushrooms, the evergreen tops forming domes that might hide anything . . . even a doctor and his assistant. If they weren't on one of these islands, they were probably dead or worse.

They circled the nearest island, but saw no signs of habitation. Pythias knew that cabins such as the one they searched for were often constructed away from the water so that the trees could be used as a windbreak and provide privacy for the occupants.

He eased the boat up between two towering rocks and let it drift in. The island was so small that he could see clear through the woods to the other side. They weren't on this island.

"Some of 'em are a lot bigger than this," he said. "We might have to get out and look around."

Jane nodded. She was about to add that it would be a

pleasure to explore the islands under different circumstances, but a low humming made her still.

They both looked up as a sleek Visitor craft sliced through the crisp autumn air. They were behind the rocks, so it wasn't likely they were sighted as the skyfighter nosed down and skimmed over the water, vanishing behind a nearby island in seconds.

Chapter 21

Jake and Charlie were scared.

"Look at them trembling like terrified rodents," Ronald said. "That is why your people will succumb to us, John Ellis—because they are weak."

Ronald turned his attention to the skyfigher's control panel, where a Visitor sat piloting the vehicle. On the screen overhead was a strangely distorted view of the ocean, as if seen through a fish-eye lens. Pine-covered islands jutted out of the water like verdant iceberg tips.

"We only wanted to go hunting," Jake moaned.

"Silence!" Ronald commanded. "You will speak only when spoken to!"

Jake cringed. Charlie had already reverted to the fetal position as they flew just a few meters over the water.

"Why did you bring these idiots to me?" Ronald demanded, turning toward John Ellis. "Are my problems not severe enough without your compounding them?"

"I . . . I thought you'd want to take them prisoner. You don't want anybody to know what's going to happen once you find the toxin, do you?"

"But we don't know anything," Charlie cried. "Just let us go back to New York and you'll never hear a word out of us again."

"If I kill you now," Ronald said, measuring his words, "I will certainly never hear another word out of you."

"Oh, please," Charlie whined. "Don't do that. We'll do anything you want."

"How did I ever let you talk me into coming to Maine on a hunting trip?" Jake asked rhetorically.

Ronald ignored them for a moment, seemingly deep in thought.

"You can do something for me," he said at length.

"Name it," Charlie said. "Anything. Anything at all, just name it."

"You came here to hunt," Ronald said, "and you will be permitted to hunt."

Jake and Charlie glanced at each other, smelling a rat but not daring to say anything. They waited for Ronald to explain what he was talking about, but they were disappointed.

"Yes," the alien captain rasped, "you will soon go hunting."

"You must stay inside, Sarah." Dr. Brunk looked at her sternly. "If they see no signs of life on the island, they might pass it by. But if they spot one of us moving about, they'll come down to investigate."

Sarah stood up and wrapped her arms around herself. "I'll go out for some firewood," she said. "If I'm just outside the door, I'll be able to hear the skyfighter before it gets close enough to see me."

"No firewood. They'll see the smoke from the air."

"What if the temperature drops tonight?" Sarah said. "What will we do then?"

"It's a chance we'll have to take. The Visitors are not playing games, and apparently they have some idea that we're on one of these islands. That means that we have to show absolutely no signs of life. If they find us here, they will take the toxin and kill us. If we destroy the toxin, they will probably torture me to find out what the formula is. They might even torture you, my dear."

Sarah saw the pain in Dr. Brunk's eyes at the very thought of such a thing. She knew that he only brought up the possibility to impress upon her the importance of staying out of sight. Dr. Brunk was not a doomsayer or alarmist. Not in the least. Sarah shuddered, imagining what the lizards might do to her. But it wasn't the first time this had occurred to her.

"We'll fight them," she said. "We'll stand up to them if they come."

"Yes, of course we will. But we might not have to. Sooner or later winter will catch up with the Visitors. If we can just hold out here until then, we'll be all right."

"But if they do find us before the resistance can intervene . . ."

"Let's not think about that, Sarah."

"Just a minute ago you said we had to consider the possibilities, and now you're telling me it's too dreadful to think about."

Dr. Brunk managed a wan smile. "I just meant that there's little sense in dwelling on it."

"Well, I think we ought to consider ways to fight them, should they get here first," Sarah said. "We have knives, a hatchet, an ax. . . ."

"And the toxin," Dr. Brunk added, "if it works."

Sarah went to him and hugged him. "It will work, Dr. Brunk. It has to."

"No, I'm afraid it could fail, Sarah."

She loved this man almost as if he were her dead father, and she refused to believe that his many months of effort in the laboratory could be in vain.

"It won't fail," she said. "I know it won't."

Chapter 22

At sunset, Pythias and Jane gave up. They returned the boat to Don Curtis' pier, thanked him, and drove the patrol car slowly up the hill.

"It's just so frustrating," Jane said. "Any bit of gossip you'd ever want to know about anybody in this town can usually be turned up just like that, but let it be something important and look what happens."

"Gossip . . ." Pythias stared grimly at the street in front of him.

"What?"

"Where do you go if you want to hear gossip?"

"Bridge club? Sewing circle? Backyard fence?"

"Or your friendly neighborhood tavern." Pythias wheeled the car onto Union Street, and a few minutes later they were entering Mike's Tavern.

The usual crowd of ne'er-do-wells were drinking the early evening away, including Herb Walsh, who greeted Pythias. Only one of the regulars was conspicuously absent, just as he had been this morning at the funeral: John Ellis.

Mike Sherman asked them what they'd have.

"Beer for me," Pythias said. "How about you, Jane?"

"Just a Coke. Diet Coke."

"Tab all right?"

"Sure."

Mike got their drinks. Pythias thought everyone was a little standoffish. Maybe they were just bashful in the presence of a lady. Still, he couldn't dismiss their hostile glances so easily. John Ellis had been doing his work, it seemed. The best thing to do about this was deal with it immediately, he decided.

"Something troubling you boys?" he asked.

Nobody said anything, but he knew he was right, especially since Herb had told him yesterday about the suspicions Ellis had tried to raise among them.

"Come on now," Pythias said. "Tell me what's on your minds."

"We don't have to talk to no traitor," a voice from one of the booths said angrily.

"Who said that?" Pythias demanded. "Come on out here and face me like a man."

A thin, lantern-jawed man of about fifty slid out of the booth and stood before Pythias.

"Arvid Ebbeson, I might have known."

"Might have known what?" Ebbeson spat.

"That you'd have plenty to say after the fighting was over."

"What's that supposed to mean?"

"Just what I said," Pythias taunted. "Where were you when we needed you a few days ago?"

"I was up the coast . . . working."

"Is that a fact?"

Red-faced and ashamed now, Ebbeson looked around him. Everyone in the place was staring at him. He stood, uncertain of whether he should fight back or sit down. Once more he glanced at Pythias. Something in the older man's expression helped him make his decision. He sat down.

"Is this what's bothering you?" Pythias said, pulling the laser pistol out from beneath his coat. He laid it on the bar.

"Fancy little doodad," Mike Sherman said, whistling. "Could we have a demonstration?"

"Set a glass down on the bar," Pythias instructed.

Mike did as he asked, gently placing a shot glass on the mahogany surface.

Pythias picked up the laser and without even aiming, fired an arc across the bar until the blue beam caught the glass. He held it there for a moment.

The glass heated, turning red, and then shattered into a thousand fragments. Smoke curled from it remains as the barflies gathered around to marvel at what they'd seen.

"Where'd you get that thing?" Melvin Grant asked.

"On my way out the door up at Brunk Labs," Pythias said. "It helped clear my path."

The men gathered around Pythias now, inclined to believe him and eager to get a better look at the laser. He passed it to the nearest of them and let them examine it.

"You didn't come up here just for target practice, did you, Sheriff?" Mike Sherman asked.

"Not exactly, Mike."

"So what can I do for you?"

"I'm trying to find out something about a real estate transaction."

Mike leaned toward him, listening.

"Seems that Dr. Brunk bought some land—an island, actually—off the coast here a little ways, but he didn't buy it under his own name."

"Mmm."

"Mrs. Snodgrass, down at city hall, thinks somebody around town made the transaction for him."

"She's right," said Mike.

"Oh, yeah? How do you know that?"

"Easy." Mike smiled broadly. "I made that deal for Dr. Brunk."

Chapter 23

Willie was dragged before Ronald, the light blinding him. He was almost grateful when a guard held his head down; the glare wasn't so harsh on the floor.

"So, my little philosopher," Ronald said. "The sun will soon rise, and we will begin our sport."

"Then you have found the place?" Willie asked.

The guard kicked him.

"No," Ronald commanded. "Let him up."

Willie was released. He stood, his eyes adjusting to the artificial light.

"Fortune is with us, Willie," Ronald grated. "Not only have we found the perfect location for our little game, but we have also located Dr. Brunk."

Willie's heart sank.

"Then you have . . ."

"We have not yet captured him," Ronald replied. "He is under surveillance and cannot possibly escape."

Willie looked down at the floor, thinking of the ritual of Zon. It wouldn't be much longer until the cold weather set in; if only they could hold out till then. But Ronald seemed so certain that the advantage was his . . . perhaps too certain. Willie sensed a weakness in Ronald's scheming mind, a lack of appreciation about how things could go awry no matter how carefully one had planned. But there was little sense in saying this to Ronald, for he would discover it eventually, in spite of himself.

"We begin to hunt at dawn," Ronald said. "You will be taken now to the site we have selected."

Ronald led the way out of the laboratory building. Following, guards surrounding him, Willie was grateful to be out in the fresh air. Though there was a slightly lower methane count than on his home world and a slightly higher nitrogen count, he had learned to enjoy breathing the air of his adopted planet. After all, he could never go home again unless the power of the military was somehow broken in his lifetime, a proposition that did not seem likely at the moment.

The only hope was Amon, the exiled spiritual leader, the being who personified the *preta-na-ma* in a mortal body. Even so, Willie could not assume that all would work out well today—for him or for the victimized human race. The poor creatures of this world might have a long struggle ahead of them, but Willie believed that they would prevail in the end. Their cause was just, and they believed in justice, thus drawing on a moral strength that eluded his people.

They walked the short distance across the parking lot to the skyfighter. The stars were out and were very clear at this high altitude. Sirius, the star around which the home world orbited, was still visible as the first gray light of dawn crept over the sea. It was the brightest star in the heavens, a gleaming jewel in the darkness that would one day be freed from the tyranny that ruled her now.

Standing before the skyfighter, they watched the ramp descend from its side. A moment later they were aboard, Willie feeling nostalgia to be on a craft similar to ones he had spent so much time on in the past. In spite of its purpose as an engine of destruction, he admired its sleek functionalism and the sophistication of its design. His people were masters of such technology. If only they would use their knowledge for constructive purposes instead of for conquest.

Ronald pointed to a seat, and Willie complied, trying

to make himself as comfortable and relaxed as possible. If he was frightened, tense, Ronald would have him at a disadvantage. But if he remained calm, then he would be a match for anyone, including the sadistic captain.

As the crew busied themselves with the details of lift-off procedure, Willie reflected that he had never been a strong individual. He had been conscripted into the military; as he had been told all through his youth, this was simply the way things were. His people had militarized their solar system and then moved out, searching always for water and food. The conventional wisdom on his world was that this armed expansion was necessary for the survival of the race. Willie had his doubts about that, but even if it were true it did not excuse the harm their way of life was doing to the humans—and to themselves, in a spiritual sense.

That, after all, was what mattered most . . . the spirit.

The skyfighter began to rise off the asphalt, the tug of gravity reversed. The strange buoyancy that he had felt so many times was welcome, even if it was to be the last time he ever felt it.

The view scan showed the buildings below and the white slashes of the breaking waves below the cliff. On the horizon, a roseate glow announced the imminent dawn.

Due to the antigravity engines, they felt nothing as the craft sped suddenly out over the water. Willie could see dark, rough shapes rising out of the surf: islands.

He expected the skyfighter to turn inland at some point, but it didn't. It followed the coast a little away and then began to slow where the islands were most densely clustered.

At last they came to rest directly over the rocky beach of an island a few kilometers wide. This, then, was the place Ronald had so carefully selected for Willie to die.

Chapter 24

Pythias Day watched the skyfighter approach the island, feeling an emotion very much like despair.

"We can't go in now," he said.

"Oh, Pyth." Jane looked as if she was about to cry.

Pythias turned the boat around before the Visitors' attention was attracted. "We need to gather a fighting force together. It's the only way we can stop them now that they're on the island."

"But who have we got left to fight them?" Jane cried. "John Ellis saw to it that all the young men were killed. There's nobody left."

"There are still people left," Pythias said. "And people will fight if their homes are threatened."

"The Visitors have taken all the fight out of them."

Pythias gunned the engine back toward the mainland. At least, he reflected, they knew where Brunk and Sarah were. Was it possible the Visitors didn't know? Perhaps they were just reconnoitering around the island by chance. There really was no outward sign that anyone was living there.

But he was kidding himself. Of course they knew—or they soon would, at any rate. They had to get some men together right away. And if there weren't enough men . . .

"Wait a minute!"

"What is it, Pyth?"

A blue blaze of energy missed Pythias' ear by a

fraction of an inch. For a moment, neither of them moved. Then Pythias pulled out his laser and turned.

Two Visitors were approaching, gliding two yards over the waves on silver disks. As they drew closer, the hum of the antigravity engines could be heard above the Evinrude. Another shot was fired, burning a neat round hole in the bow.

Pythias fired back, the bolt flying a little wide of the nearest Visitor. The two disks began to zigzag.

"They're just trying to scare us away," Pythias shouted. "But I'm gonna have to kill them. Once their leader hears about this laser, he'll know it's me, even if these two don't."

The two disk riders were slowing down, perhaps considering turning back.

"Hold this!" Pythias tossed the laser pistol to Jane and brought the prow around 180 degrees. Cold salt spray in his face, he gunned the motor, directing the boat toward the two Visitors. He saw their mouths open in astonishment under their dark glasses as he attacked.

Jane didn't wait for Pythias to take the laser back. She squeezed off a shot that seared the air between the two disks. The next one barely missed one of the disk riders, who almost fell off in his efforts to get out of the way. His partner laid down a barrage of laser fire, boiling the seawater around the boat but leaving Pythias and Jane untouched.

Pythias struggled to the front of the boat, clapping his hand onto Jane's shoulder.

"Go back and pilot the boat," he shouted over the engine, the disks, and the buzzing laser fire. "I'm used to this thing."

He took the laser as Jane clambered into the stern. Taking careful aim, he fired, narrowly missing the nearest Visitor. He kept his finger on the trigger instead of just squeezing off a burst, and swept his fire across the horizon, as he had done in the bar when he destroyed the shot glass.

His slice took down the Visitor, who screamed in pain and horror as he toppled from his mount. He disappeared in an explosion of white foam.

"Good shooting, Pyth!" Jane shouted encouragingly.

The second Visitor pivoted on his disk, trying to get away from them now. He was headed away from the island, desperate to escape his prey-turned-hunter.

Firing wildly behind him, the Visitor soared higher, trying to get out of range. He lost ground performing this maneuver, however.

Pythias squinted into the sun and burned a blue arc across the sky, just missing the disk rider as he swerved, leaning perilously to one side thirty feet above the water.

Pythias lost sight of him for a moment and then realized that the crafty alien had swung around behind them. He jumped up, nearly capsizing the boat. The Visitor was coming right at them from behind, firing wildly, no more than three feet over the wave crests.

A burst of laser fire just missed Jane, and she recoiled in terror. The shot struck the gunwale and exploded in a shower of sparks. Even if he didn't shoot them, the son of a bitch would sink the boat, thought Pythias.

I can't afford to miss this time, Pythias told himself. He's getting too close to miss us. The disk glided steadily above the waves, unlike the bouncing boat.

Pythias took aim, and so did the Visitor. For an instant they stared stright down the barrels of their lasers into each other's eyes. The Visitor hesitated.

Pythias could see nothing but the reflection of Jane's terrified face in the alien's dark glasses.

He fired.

The alien shuddered. His clawed fingers went limp, and he dropped the gun into the ocean. An instant later, he followed.

Pythias and Jane watched the disk veer off and knife into the water. Climbing into the back of the boat, Pythias embraced Jane and grabbed the rudder.

"Pyth . . ."

"Yes, Jane?"

He expected her to break down and cry, but what she said surprised him.

"We better get away from here before they send more soldiers after us."

Chapter 25

"Come on, boys," John Ellis called to the two flagging hunters. He waited a few moments for them to catch up, and then scolded them for their slackness.

"We never wanted to come out to this island," Charlie said, breathing heavily from his exertions. "We wanted to hunt on the mainland."

"Don't worry," John said, smiling wickedly. "There's good hunting out on this island. Excellent hunting."

"Deer?" Charlie asked.

"No deer, but bear, rabbits . . . lots of things."

"There are bear out here?" Jake asked, incredulous. "Oh, no!"

"Take it easy, Jake," Charlie admonished him. "We've got guns, haven't we?"

"He's right, you know," Ellis said. "Bear meat's good, and just imagine the rug you'll have when you get back to New York."

Jake and Charlie glanced at each other. Without saying so, they had both come to the same conclusion. They were not going back to New York, even if they did what the Visitors wanted. Why the Visitors hadn't just killed them and let it go at that, they had no idea. The fact that they hadn't was the only thing that gave them any hope at all.

"Come on," Ellis said. He led them through the woods, speaking softly as he went. "The bears are usually either fishing or having lunch in a blueberry patch."

"Just so they don't decide to have *us* for lunch," Jake replied.

John Ellis chuckled. "This way," he said, leading them into an open space where bushes grew widly, festooned with blueberries.

"Go on in and take a look," he said to Charlie.

Charlie looked at Jake, who shrugged.

"Okay," Charlie said, and made his way steadily toward the bushes.

His eyes darting around, Charlie saw no movement except for a few dead leaves drifting down from the boughs. He heard nothing but the wind gently moving the branches. It looked safe enough.

Glancing back at his companions, he saw Ellis gesticulating at him to go deeper into the blueberry patch. He was inclined to ignore the traitorous bastard, but he didn't really dare to. There was no way they were going to escape from the Visitors, and he didn't want Ellis to prejudice them against him. There was always a chance the Visitors would let them go once they tired of playing with them.

Suddenly Charlie felt something grab the sleeve of his hunting jacket, right at the cuff. Terrified, he tried to pull himself free, but he couldn't seem to. Sweat pouring form his forehead, he turned to face the thing that had him in its grasp.

There was nothing there.

Charlie looked down and saw what it was. It wasn't a bear, but a branch that had caught his sleeve. He worked it free in disgust and determinedly made his way deeper into the blueberry thicket.

After a few minutes, he thought he heard something. It was a low, whuffing noise. He held perfectly still. No sound except the wind through the trees. That wasn't what he'd heard, was it? After a few more seconds, he started moving again, his 30.06 at the ready.

It must have only been the wind, he decided. There was nothing in here. Growing more and more assured, he poked at the tangled undergrowth with his rifle barrel. Probing with the gun, he slowly advanced deeper and deeper into the thicket. He was actually beginning to enjoy himself, fearlessly rummaging about in a den of wild bears.

Something grabbed the rifle from inside the bushes.

"Whoa," Charlie breathed. He had thought a bear had him once; the barrel was probably just stuck on a branch or something.

He attempted to pry it loose.

The whuffing noise came out of the bushes again, right from where the rifle was stuck. Charlie tried to fire, but the 30.06's safety was on. He carefully reached down and released it.

Just as he was about to fire, the bushes heaved and an enormous black bear emerged, roaring ferociously. Charlie looked into those gaping jaws just as he tumbled backward into the bushes behind him. The rifle went off in a terrific explosion, deafening Charlie as he flailed in the bushes.

He managed to scramble to his feet, running for all he was worth toward Jake and Ellis. He saw them staring in disbelief as he tried to catch up with them.

Glancing over his shoulder, Charlie saw the bear charging at him, its massive limbs churning through the snapping branches. It roared angrily as he dug into the humus underneath the dead leaves and ran for cover.

He caught Jake and Charlie a few seconds later, moving past them so quickly they seemed to be standing still. If human hair could really stand on end, Charlie's would have done so now. He didn't stop running until he reached the rocky beach.

Chapter 26

"Did you hear a shot?" Dr. Brunk asked, going to the window.

"Yes, I think so." Sarah cocked her head, listening for another rifle report. She waited thirty second and heard nothing further.

"Maybe it was thunder," she said.

"No, thunder never sounded like that," Dr. Brunk observed. "Besides, look out that window. There isn't a cloud in the sky."

"Then they've found us."

"Maybe, but I don't think that was the Visitors."

"Who, then?"

"I don't know. Hunters wouldn't come all the way out here ordinarily, not when there's so much game on the mainland."

"Unless they heard about the bears." Sarah grinned and squeezed Dr. Brunk's hand as he moved away from the window. "It must be hunters who've come out here looking for bears, Dr. Brunk. And that means the Visitors must have cleared out of the area."

"Don't be too sure," Dr. Brunk advised. "It could be a trick."

Sarah became subdued. "You're right. I was ready to go running out there and welcome them with open arms. I have to learn to be more realistic."

"You've been isolated here for days on end," Dr. Brunk said. "I certainly can't blame you if you're a little antsy. Nevertheless, I must insist that you stay inside until we're sure there's no danger."

Sarah wondered if they would ever be out of danger, now that the Visitors had come. If they could only hold out until the weather got colder. The toxin in Earth's ecosystem turned out to work in cold climates, where the bacteria went into a dormant stage in winter, becoming active in the Spring thaw. The toxin burned itself out in hot climates, where it was unable to go into a dormant stage. The Visitors would die if they stayed past the first frost . . . unless they had the antidote Nathan Bates had developed for friendly aliens like the one who had been coming to help Dr. Brunk. The Visitors could easily have analyzed the Red Dust and the antidote if some had fallen into their clutches. Given their superior technology it was even possible they had developed it without a sample of the antitoxin. That was why Dr. Brunk's works was so important. That was why they must survive.

"We're out of food," Dr. Brunk said.

"Good," Sarah replied. "We can both stand to lose a few pounds."

Dr. Brunk smiled. "I suppose so."

Neither of them wanted to say it aloud, but both feared that the Visitors were closing in on them. The pleasant Indian Summer temperatures had been working against them, making their chances of survival most unlikely. Somehow, each hoped that if such despair were not uttered, there might yet be some hope—a slim hope, but a hope nonetheless.

Dr. Brunk sat down in the filthy old armchair. He put his pipe to his mouth and searched for matches. Sarah went to the mantel and took a box of kitchen matches to him.

"Thank you," Dr. Brunk said, lighting his pipe.

"Do you remember how worried I was that it would get cold a couple of days ago?" she asked.

"Yes."

"Now I wish it would freeze," she said. "Freeze solid and kill those goddamn lizards."

"We might die too, Sarah."

"It wouldn't matter. Somebody would find the new toxin here with our bodies, and the world would at least have a weapon to fight them with."

Against her will, tears welled up and ran down her cheeks. She turned away from Dr. Brunk and sank into the old sofa on the other side of the cabin's tiny living room.

Dr. Brunk removed the pipe stem from his mouth. "Oh, Sarah," he said, "I'm so sorry. I never thought it would turn out like this."

He went to her and sat down, holding her hand. "It's hard, I know. But we didn't have any choice but to flee when we heard the Visitors were coming. We've done the best we could, and now we have to hope things are going to work out somehow."

Sarah dried her tears, thankful at least for Dr. Brunk's sympathy. The she noticed something. "Dr. Brunk, listen," she said.

"What is it, Sarah? I don't hear anything."

"That's just it. Usually the birds are very noisy this time of day, but there isn't a sound coming from outside this cabin."

Dr. Brunk rose and went to the door. He quietly opened it and looked out into the little clearing and the forest beyond. "You're right," he said. "It's completely silent. I don't see so much as a chipmunk moving out there either."

Sarah tried to hide her terror, but she knew Dr. Brunk could see it. She saw it in his eyes too.

"I've never known this to happen out here," he said lamely.

"That's because nothing like this has happened before," Sarah replied.

"Sarah, don't jump to conclusions. It might not be anything. . . ."

"They're coming, Dr. Brunk," Sarah said, cowering on the sofa. "They're coming for us now."

Chapter 27

Willie stood on the beach, Visitor guards all around him as he faced Ronald, the forest just a few meters behind him.

"I am going to set you free now, Willie," Ronald said. "I have not treated you badly in the past few days so that you would have your wits and physical agility today. You will have this entire island as your playing field. It is not very large, perhaps a dozen kilometers across, and there are, shall we say, obstacles, but there are also things that you might use to your advantage, if you remain calm and logical."

Willie nodded, noting how uniform the circle of guards was, a perfect geometric shape surrounding him and their master. It was the prelude of the *ninj-ki-ra*, the ritual of death. He had never witnessed it before, but it was legendary on the home world. An ancient tradition, the *ninj-ki-ra* was now practiced only by the military, and only in extreme cases involving treason. Undoubtedly, Ronald was stretching the rules by invoking it in Willie's case, but it probably didn't seem so to him.

"You understand what you must do?" Ronald asked him now.

"Yes," Willie said. "I must try to survive."

"And you know what that means, don't you, my little philosopher?"

Willie shook his head.

"You must kill me—" Ronald's reptilian mouth split

into a grin, his forked tongue sliding out as he savored
this moment. "—if you can."

That would be Ronald's ultimate triumph of course.
Willie perceived that the captain feared the *preta-na-ma*.
He would replace it with this game of murder, or, in the
unlikely event he died himself, turn Willie into a
murderer. Thus he would invalidate the principles to
which Willie now devoted his life—or so he believed.

"Though you will hunt me like a wild beast," Willie
said, looking straight into Ronald's eyes through the
inscrutable dark glasses, "I will not attempt to kill you."

"Then you will die," Ronald grated, his voice rising
over the lapping waves.

"Perhaps, but only my body will be dead. My spirit
will live on."

Ronald hissed in rage, furious that he had not yet
broken Willie.

"We will see how much of you lives," Ronald said.
"Go now!"

Willie took one last look at his nemesis and turned
around. The soldier behind him stepped back, breaking
the crimson circle of soldiers to let him pass.

Willie moved forward one pace. He hesitated for a
second, and then passed out of the broken circle. The
game had begun.

Running toward the shelter of the forest, he glanced
over his shoulder. The circle of Visitors had not moved.
As Ronald promised, he would wait thirty minutes
before entering the forest. Willie would have time to
hide, at least, and time to think about some sort of
defense against Ronald's weapons.

He welcomed the enveloping darkness as he entered
the woods. Trees with white bark soon gave way to larger
pines. Willie had seen the latter in California, but the
white trees were unfamiliar. How much there was to
learn, and now there was very little chance that he would

ever have another opportunity to educate himself on the flora and fauna of his adopted planet.

There was little time for anything now except thoughts of survival.

Tiny, bushy-tailed mammals scurried out of his way as he ran—squirrels, if he remembered correctly. His footsteps pounded noisily across the carpet of dead leaves. He didn't know where to go, only that he should get as far away from Ronald as possible.

If Ronald were to observe the *ninj-ki-ra* to the letter, as Willie believed he would, the guards would remain behind. Only Ronald himself would hunt Willie. If Ronald could be defeated, then Willie would be exonerated. He would be expected to return to his people, of course, in that unlikely event. But that would be an impossibility; he had cast his lot with the people on Earth. His ethics forbade him to turn his back on them, no matter what the consequences.

Willie labored heavily, running while he wore human garb and the pseudo skin. He would make better progress if he wore nothing but his own skin.

He stopped, leaning one hand against the rough bark of a pine tree. It was warm enough, though he knew that the temperature could drop very rapidly this far north. Even in Los Angeles, there were times when he was grateful for the thermal protection of the pseudo skin. Nevertheless, he must chance going on without it now, for he could not allow it to slow him down.

Removing his jacket and trousers, he began to peel away the artificial human epidermis.

Chapter 28

Slowly and elegantly, Willie pulled one fingertip at a time free. He then perforated the pseudo skin around the wrists, using the calcium-carbonate fingernails of one hand, and as soon as he had pulled off the skin like a glove, the claws on his own hand.

Using the same method, he cut open the front of the pseudo skin with a talon from the collarbone to the groin. Next, he pulled the false neck away from his green, armored flesh, skillfully stretching the pliable material until he was able to pull the face over his head like a mask. He couldn't afford to concern himself with the visual scanners that served as eyes, expensive and delicate as they were. One of them popped out onto the leaf-strewn humus and vanished as he pulled his legs, ankles, and finally his feet out of the pseudo skin he had not taken off since he had come to live among humans.

Discarding the pseudo skin under a bush, Willie stretched his limbs in a way that he had almost forgotten, his posture at such times was so alarming to humans. It was good to be physically free at last, even under these less than ideal circumstances. Exhilarated, Willie began to move deeper into the forest, searching as he ran for some means of slowing down Ronald.

Which way should he go? Perhaps it didn't matter, as long as he didn't leave an obvious trail that Ronald could pick up easily. It would probably be best to take some of the more difficult paths, for if he followed the more accessible routes, Ronald would surely be right behind him. Willie jumped into a thicket, the sticklike branches lashing his skin.

Here he had the advantage over a human, his horny hide shielding the sensitive tissue underneath his scales for the most part, though the soft underparts of his arms and legs suffered a stinging laceration from time to time. Still, it was not intolerable pain and did not slow him down significantly. He gritted his teeth, realizing they were the false human teeth that went with his terrestrial disguise. He tugged at them as he crashed through the bushes. The dentures were designed to interlock with his fangs, but he worked them free in a few moments and tossed them into the underbrush.

The false teeth met with a terrifying roar as they landed. Willie was rooted to the spot, unable to move at all in the presence of such a fearsome noise. Standing as still as a statue, he peered into the thicket to see what manner of creature he had stirred by the ill-timed toss of the teeth.

An enormous beast lumbered toward him, huge and black and hairy, with imposing claws and fangs. It rolled forward on its powerful legs like an engine of destruction.

Willie's heart leaped up into his gullet at the sight of the monster. His first impulse was to run for all he was worth, but somehow he remembered the *preta-na-ma*, sensing that he would not escape the creature's clutches by fleeing.

Willie stood his ground, facing the huge animal.

This surprised it. It slowed its pace until it was barely moving at all. The brute was of the family Ursidae, Willie was quite sure. He had read about bears in illustrated books; fascinating creatures. Why did it want to attack him?

He attempted to communicate with it through the

preta-na-ma. At the sound of the chanting, the bear's ears picked up. It sidled up to Willie and sniffed his claws inquisitively.

Still chanting, Willie reached out and touched its enormous head. The chant rippled through Willie's body and passed through his mind into the bear's skull. Tongue lolling, the great beast allowed Willie to stroke it.

"We know each other now, my friend," Willie said. "You can share your troubles with me."

Closing his eyes and concentrating, Willie saw a darkness, unadulterated by the slightest hint of color or light . . . and then there was a glimmer . . . a vision of a dark cave surrounded by a thick undergrowth . . . and inside the cave there were the bear's young.

"Ah," said Willie, "you are a mother protecting your young from intruders."

The female bear made a soft mewling sound as Willie petted her. She licked his open claw.

Willie looked further into her rudimentary mind. He saw that there were tiny fruits on the wild bushes that formed much of the bears' subsistence. Reaching out, Willie plucked a few from a branch and fed them to her.

As she ate, he projected a desire to see her cubs. The bear hesitated for a moment and then lumbered off into the bushes in the direction from which she had come. Willie followed her, snapping branches to make his way easier.

Willie reflected that he had never communicated with an animal so successfully. He attributed it to his heightened perception due to the *preta-na-ma*.

Almost hidden by the bushes was the cave mouth. After the mother, Willie crawled inside and was greeted by three frightened bear cubs. The mother nuzzled and licked them, and after a few moments they were calmed. Willie picked a few berries and fed them.

"I must go now," he said after the cubs had eaten out of his hand. "If I stay here, the one who hunts me might kill you too."

The bears made a sad honking sound, which Willie heard for a few minutes as he moved off into the woods again.

Chapter 29

It was time. Ronald stepped through the circle of guards and started into the forest. His soldiers were under strict orders not to follow.

In his lightweight, armored uniform, Ronald would be well protected; only his head would be a target. His tongue lashed into the cool autumn air as he considered how likely Willie's chances were.

Ronald hoped this one would at least try to fight. In the past, he had conducted the *ninj-ki-ra* on a handful of planets. It was always enjoyable, and always a good way to keep the troops in line. But he had to admit to himself that there was more to it than that. He found the traitor's embracing of the *preta-na-ma* disturbing. It was of course against the law to practice the old religion, and now Ronald saw why. It superseded one's love for one's planet, one's people, and it permitted the weak to rationalize treason as a spiritual awakening, as Willie had done. It was unconscionable, intolerable. Willie would have to pay the price for his folly.

Such things were not permitted in the great city of Tontran, Ronald reflected as he moved aside a branch with his laser pistol. But when he was little more than an eggling, he had gone to the provinces with his guardian, and there he had seen elderly ones practicing the *preta-na-ma*. His guardian had yanked him away from the forbidden spectacle, later explaining to him the evils of the old beliefs.

Why did the *preta-na-ma* refuse to die? Now it had

even come across space and reared its ugly head on Earth.

It would take great strength to stamp it out, but it would be done. He would initiate the task today, with the destruction of Willie.

And if Willie fought back, so much the better. Not only because it would provide superior sport, but it would also prove the shallowness of the superstitions. It was all very well to speak of nonviolence and dying before taking another's life—until you were actually faced with the possibility of death because of those very beliefs. He would soon see how strong Willie's faith was.

Ronald winced as a shaft of light penetrated his dark glasses. His world, with its thicker layer of carbon dioxide, was easier on the eyes, though a little warmer than Earth. Still, it was remarkable that they had found a planet so close to Sirius with a breathable atmosphere and so much water. Surely the adherents of the *preta-na-ma* could see that it was divinely ordained, he thought sardonically.

Tiny mammals with enormous bushy tails jumped out of his way without so much as a sound. Ronald admired their agility; he would imitate it in the hunt.

He spied a depression in the leaves. Willie had been here, or a human . . . perhaps it was Dr. Brunk, his ultimate quarry. Willie had no way of knowing he was so close to the man he had come to Cutter's Cove seeking, and now he would lead Ronald to Dr. Brunk. What delicious irony.

Ronald squatted to examine the track. It appeared to be leading to the right. Willie must have decided to follow a more difficult path than the one Ronald was on now. Soon a broken branch confirmed Ronald's suspicion. It would be easier to follow Willie now than if he had kept moving straight through the forest.

"You make the hunt too simple," Ronald said aloud.

He started into the thick underbrush but soon lost his way. He found no more traces of his prey.

Forced to double back, Ronald returned to the spot where he had found the footprint. Perhaps Willie was more clever than he'd thought, Ronald speculated. His trail led into the bushes and disappeared. The undergrowth was simply too heavy to follow.

Perhaps Ronald should circle around the bushes. It would take Willie some time and considerable effort to fight his way through, and then only to find Ronald waiting for him when he emerged on the other side.

Ronald clucked his tongue at the thought of it. How very amusing . . . if it worked.

He stepped softly through the leaves, starting to work his way around the bushes, which appeared to be nearly a kilometer wide.

Something caught his eye. Ronald turned and leveled his laser at it. A patch of tan, the same color as Willie's jacket, behind a lone bush outside the thicket.

Was the game to end so quickly then?

"Come out!" Ronald commanded.

There was no response from behind the bush.

"I know you're there," Ronald barked. "Now come out before I shoot!"

The thing behind the bush didn't stir. Ronald squeezed off a warning shot next to the bush. A tuft of white smoke swirled into the air and vanished, but Willie did not come out from behind the bush.

Ronald moved closer, until he was standing less than a meter from the bush. He knew Willie couldn't charge him while he was armed. Was Willie dead?

Ronald bounded over the bush, pointing his laser at what he thought would be Willie. Instead, he found the clothes his quarry had been wearing, and the shredded remains of a human pseudo skin.

Ronald laughed. "So he goes naked in the woods now, like the child the *preta-na-ma* tells him to emulate."

And though he could not quite admit it to himself as he continued stalking Willie, the prospect disturbed him. Willie was not playing the game the way Ronald had hoped he would,

Chapter 30

John Ellis looked at his watch, suddenly realizing that he should have been back on the beach minutes ago. Ronald had specified that only the two New Yorkers were to be in the woods once the chase begin. Far be it form John Ellis to question the head lizard's authority.

"Good hunting, boys," he said. "This is where we part company."

Jake and Charlie looked at him suspiciously, as if they didn't really believe he was through busting their chops.

"Well," Ellis said, "aren't you going to say good-bye?" He couldn't resist a parting shot. "After all, we may never see each other again."

It pleased him to see their frightened, confused expressions. Pulling the visor of his cap over his eyes, he grinned maliciously and left them standing awkwardly holding their rifles.

"See you around," he said.

He had only gone a few paces when Jake called after him, "Hey!"

Ellis hesitated, turning to see what the pathetic fool wanted.

"What are we suppose to do now?" Jake asked, his voice pleading.

"Stand there and whine, for all I care," Ellis said. "Or do some hunting."

"But why?" Jake pleaded. "Why did they send us out here?"

"Don't ask me," Ellis said, starting back into the woods again. "The Lord works in mysterious ways."

Watching Ellis until he vanished, the two friends stood mournfully, both wishing they were back home now instead of marooned on this island with a bunch of lizards and a bear.

"So aren't you going to tell me how lucky we are to be here?" Jake said at last.

"Don't be a wise guy," Charlie replied. "We're both in this together."

"That's true. I wish I could just call a cab and go home, but I'm stuck here with you, like it or not."

"Well, then," Charlie said, his face breaking into a grin, "let's do what the man said. Let's go hunting."

"Go hunting! What if the Visitors are hunting us?"

"Would they have given us our guns if they were hunting us?"

Jake mulled that over. "Maybe not," he allowed at last. "All right, so we'll hunt. We'll hunt already."

"I knew you'd see things my way."

"Let's get started," Jake said. "The sun is getting higher all the time."

"Right."

The two men stood staring at each other.

"Well?" Jake said at last.

"Well, let's split up," Charlie said. "Yeah, that's it. Let's split up."

"Why?" Jake asked suspiciously.

"Because we'll be covering twice as much ground."

"And we won't be making as much noise without each other to yell at."

"Yeah, that's right, Jake," Charlie said. "It'll be better if we split up."

"Just like at the office," Jake said.

Charlie looked around, peering into the woods to the

right and left of them. "I'll go this way," he said after a few seconds.

"How come?"

"No particular reason," Charlie admitted. "It just looks like it might be better hunting over there."

"Why?"

"I don't know . . . just an intuition."

"Okay, Jungle Jim," Jake said. "You go that way, and I'll go this way. I'll meet you back here in two hours."

They synchronized their watches. Jake went one way and Charlie the other, though neither was sure if he was headed north, south, east, or west.

Jake picked his way through the brush, mumbling to himself lugubriously. He felt that if he always expected the worst, he would never be disappointed. Usually something less than the worst happened, but this trip things were getting dangerously close to the limit.

Every few minutes he stopped to listen, hearing the rat-tat-tat of a woodpecker or the chittering of a squirrel. At least the gnats weren't too thick, as they had been the last time he'd gone hunting.

Nearly forty-five minutes had passed when Jake heard something moving in the bushes behind him. He froze, and then very slowly turned around.

Nothing moved.

Was it the bear? Or something else? Jake's first impulse was to tell it to come out, but that would be stupid. It would probably get away if he did that. The thing to do was to wait for it to move again so he could get a shot at it.

As quietly as possible, Jake released the safety and stood his ground.

Chapter 31

Strangely, Willie felt at home in the forest. He was more aware of his body than he had been since he was a child at play in the desert of his own planet. The cool, yet comfortable temperature seemed to help, as well as the sheer variety of life on the island. From insects to bears, the place teemed with vibrant, active creatures. The horned ridges on Willie's forehead trembled as he received signals of their life forces. He was attuned to their world now as he had never been before, trusting in the power of the *preta-na-ma* and the communion of life throughout the universe to guide him through treacherous and difficult times. And yet he could not be certain that his instincts were any better than Ronald's here in this strange forest on an alien world.

He heard something moving through the trees near the edge of the blueberry patch and lowered himself as close to the ground as he could, his sinews taut as he prepared himself for probable violence.

The creature came nearer, whatever it was, crashing and thudding through the brush in a way that suggested to Willie that it was human and not an animal. Willie could feel it approaching as much as he heard it, his body stretching out in a reptile crouch that made his green skin blend in with his surroundings. For a moment or two, Willie wondered what he would do if he had to struggle with the man; in his fear, might he not spit his poisonous venom on his assailant without intending to? It might kill the man, but would Willie be accountable? Even now, his life endangered, these difficult moral questions perplexed him.

Willie saw the man through the bushes. He wore a colored jacket and cap so bright Willie could hardly stand to look at it. More disturbing than that, however, was the rifle the man held. Willie sensed his nervousness, not a reassuring perception under the circumstances. Still, Willie had only to hold still and the hunter would pass by.

The hunter paused for a moment and looked around. He seemed to have no idea that anyone was watching him as he scratched his head with his free hand and cradled the rifle with the other.

After a few seconds he moved on. Willie slowly rose and walked the last few meters out of the blueberry patch. He entered the woods, welcoming its cool, dark protection. He had crossed the best part of a kilometer through thick bushes to end up here, and he hoped Ronald wouldn't know it.

Watching for movement from the woods, Willie wondered how the hunter had come to be on the island. Was Ronald behind this too, adding more spice to the recipe?

Circling the blueberry patch from the shelter of woods, Willie's keen senses were attuned to the slightest nuance. It was not difficult for him to find the second human hunter. This one was a heavier man, dressed more or less the same way and carrying an equally formidable looking rifle.

Willie decided to follow this one. It was a simple matter, even when the fellow was briefly out of sight; his noisy progress was discernible from a fairly sizable distance. What was even more remarkable, he was slowly turning back the way he'd come, apparently without realizing it.

This meant that he would ultimately cross the path of

the other hunter. If Willie were to continue circling, he
too would soon encounter the first one, but if he remained unseen, perhaps there was something he could do
to discourage them from trespassing here on the playing
field of the *ninj-ki-ra*, the province of death.

He moved deeper into the woods and started back the
way he had come, sprinting when he came to an open
spot between the trees. Calculating where the first hunter
would be by now, given his position when Willie had last
seen him, Willie soon caught up with him. He knew the
second hunter couldn't be far behind.

Spying a little mound at the edge of the woods, Willie
climbed it and crouched low to the ground. Virtually
invisible from the border of the blueberry patch, he
waited.

The second hunter came into view, meandering along,
looking puzzled that he had somehow come back to the
blueberry patch. A few moments later, the other one
showed up. Willie's position gave him a flawless vantage
point.

Clutching a stone in a taloned hand, he threw it
midway between the two hunters, who were hidden from
each other by the mound and the thick clusters of pine
and spruce growing on this part of the island.

He saw them both start in terror at the sound of the
rock clunking to the ground.

Almost as one, the two hunters lifted their rifles to
their shoulders and fired. Their booming rifle shots
echoed through the forest, making a terrific racket.

Each hunter heard the rifle report of the other, cringed,
and turned tail and ran away.

Willie waited until he could no longer hear their boots
clomping through the dead leaves, and then stood. He
was thankful that the two hunters hadn't hurt one
another. He hoped that they would return to the mainland

now. If not, a dangerous new element was added to the game.

Just now, though, he had other worries. It was best to get away from this part of the island, now that shots had been fired. Ronald would not be far away.

Chapter 32

The shooting had been much closer this time. Dr. Brunk knew it wouldn't be long before they were besieged here in the little cabin.

"I'd better destroy the toxin," he said, staring at the cold fireplace. "And the antidote."

Sarah jumped to her feet. "You can't do that! Not after all your work."

"I can't let it fall into their hands," Dr. Brunk said. "Scientific discoveries have a way of coming along about the same time, but independently. Most likely, it won't be long before someone comes up with the toxin. But if the Visitors already have it, they'll be one more step ahead of us."

Sarah hung her head, realizing that she had allowed emotion to overcome logic at a crucial time. "I'm sorry."

"Oh, Sarah," Dr. Brunk said kindly. "You're like a daughter to me, you know." He went to her and put his arm around her shoulder.

"Can't we wait just a little longer? If you destroy the toxin now and the resistance gets here in time to drive the Visitors away like they did before . . ."

Dr. Brunk's hand touched the nearest of the tiny crystalline vials. "Perhaps you're right, Sarah. We'll wait."

She could tell from his tired eyes that he was only humoring her, that he believed they were doomed. If he were alone, he might even consider suicide. Thank God she was with him.

"I wonder how my mother is doing," Sarah said, just to change the subject.

Dr. Brunk seemed to perk up a little at the mention of her mother. Indeed, Sarah had always hoped to get the two of them together. Maybe if they survived all this, there was still a chance.

"The Visitors probably haven't attacked Cutter's Cove again," Dr. Brunk said. "So she's probably okay—at least I hope so."

"It must be nerve-racking for her to see skyfighters flying impudently over these islands. She's always hated situations she couldn't do anything to change. For her to just sit there helplessly and watch . . ."

At that moment, they heard the crack of another rifle report.

"You fool!" Ronald grated, wrenching the gun out of Charlie's hands.

"I'm sorry," Charlie whined. "When you tapped me on the shoulder, the gun just went off."

A shower of leaves fell from the branch Charlie's ill-timed shot had blown off an elm tree.

"Your shooting led me to you," Ronald said. "What were you firing at?"

"I don't know," Charlie admitted. "I never saw it. I only heard it clunking around."

"Did you hit anything?"

"I don't know—and I didn't stick around long enough to find out."

Ronald was amused in spite of himself. It was this cowardly streak in humans that encouraged him to believe that his people would ultimately subdue this planet. For every Pythias Day, there was one like this cringing mass of quivering fear. But where was the human's companion?

"The other," Ronald demanded. "Where is he?"

"I haven't seen him in a while. We were gonna meet at the edge of the blueberry patch, but I haven't been able to find the exact spot."

Shaking his massive head, Ronald thrust the gun back into Charlie's hands. "Continue the hunt," he said.

Charlie examined the still-smoking barrel. "Do I have to?" he asked.

"You came here to hunt, did you not?"

Charlie shook his head. "I think I've hunted enough."

An ominous clicking sound came from Ronald's throat. Beneath his fanged jaws, the loose flesh swelled like a balloon. "You will do as I say," he rasped.

"Y-Yes, sir." Charlie backed away.

Before he vanished in the forest, Ronald called after him: "In which direction did you last see your companion?"

Charlie looked around. "I think it was . . . that way." He pointed off into the woods.

"Very good. Remember, there are dangerous beasts on this island. Shoot at anything that moves."

Charlie looked at him dubiously. "Anything?"

"Anything."

Forlornly, Charlie moved off into the woods again.

Ronald snarled. He was quite certain that the series of rifle shots involving Charlie had also involved Jake. And he was fairly confident that Willie had been the cause of it. The traitor was more clever than he would have guessed, but in the end that would only make the kill sweeter for Ronald. He was closing in on Willie, and on Dr. Brunk too, but Dr. Brunk could wait. For now, the hunt was on for Willie, and it promised to be more exciting than Ronald could have ever guessed.

Chapter 33

It sounded to John Ellis as if there was some action going on somewhere on the island. All those shots must have meant something. Tramping through the woods now, he hoped to find Ronald soon in order to find out if the girl was still alive. Ronald had promised her to him. Well, at least he had suggested that he'd give it some thought.

A partridge whirred out of the bushes, vanishing in the treetops. John didn't have enough time to take a shot at it. Had Ronald blasted Willie already, or was all the shooting just those two clowns from New York blasting away at anything that moved? Maybe he should move farther inland to see if he could find out.

The more he thought about possessing Sarah Foley, the more excited he got. He remembered her as a cheerleader in high school, all the guys lusting after her. She never even knew he existed, and even if she did, she probably laughed at him along with her sosh crowd.

She wouldn't be laughing when he got his hands on her. Nobody would laugh at him ever again. He would have a whole town to lord it over, not just a few drunks down at Mike's who feared him because he could kick their asses. They would all fear him from now on, even respect him. That would be something new—respect.

Ellis came on a large rock jutting out of the ground at a sharp angle. It occurred to him that he could see quite a bit of the forest from the top of it if he were to climb up there.

Stopping for a few moments, he pulled a flask from inside his hunting jacket and took a snort. Smacking his lips and sighing deeply, he put the booze away and started around the back of the rock. He climbed to the top and sat watching the forest floor. From here, he could see even more than he had anticipated. If anybody moved within fifty yards, he wouldn't be able to miss them.

Taking the flask out again, John took another hit. Sitting cross-legged, he waited, drinking and listening to the sounds of the forest and the distant sounds of the sea. The weather was so nice and warm, it was hard to imagine what the next few weeks would bring. There were those who said the coming cold weather would drive away the Visitors, but John didn't believe it. Even if they did have to leave, it would only be temporary. Why didn't everybody see how inevitable it was that the lizards were going to take over? One ride in that skyfighter and all doubt had been removed from his mind.

When the Visitors had nabbed him that night, just walking down an alley to take a leak on the way home, he thought they were going to kill him. Instead, they took him to Ronald.

He had promised Ronald that he would be his eyes and ears in the village, and Ronald had accepted—without the threat of conversion.

No one could accuse John Ellis of not playing the percentages.

John dozed, one ear open to any unusual sounds. At last his sleeping mind heard something, and he awakened in an instant.

The forest was still for a moment, and then the chirping and twittering began to pick up again. Something had disturbed the animals and insects for a moment, though. Ellis was sure of it.

And then he spotted the cause of the disturbance.

Something crouched low to the ground, something that moved with an unearthly grace.

He had never seen a Visitor completely unclothed before. Its movements were quick, furtive, its scaly skin and ridged back dazzling in the shafts of sunlight. The hornlike extrusions on its forehead trembled above its gleaming, intelligent eyes.

This must be the one Ronald was looking for. Ellis smiled, thinking what a feather this would be in his cap if he captured the renegade alien.

Ellis got Willie in his sights. "Hold it right there," he said, "or I'll blow a hole in you the size of Aroostook County."

Willie froze. He sensed that an escape attempt would only lead to death. His only hope was to reason with the man. "I mean you no charm," he said in English.

"No *charm*?" Ellis said. "You mean *harm*, don't you?"

"Yes, I mean you no harm."

John Ellis rose and made his way down the side of the boulder, careful to keep his rifle aimed at Willie. "Well, whether you mean any harm or not, fella, Ronald's gonna be glad to see you."

Clearly, this man did not understand the *ninj-ki-ra*. "You cannot do this," Willie said.

"Oh, can't I?" Ellis approached him, pulling out a long piece of twine he kept in his pocket for emergencies. "Watch me."

He gestured for Willie to back up until the alien's ridged back was against a birch tree. Willie was tied securely to the trunk in a matter of seconds.

"Now, then," Ellis said, stepping back to admire his handiwork, "I reckon I'll see if I can't find Ronald. He'll probably want to use you for a little target practice, old chum."

Chapter 34

As John Ellis disappeared into the woods, Willie tugged at his bonds. It was no good; he couldn't seem to loosen them at all. The more he struggled, the tighter the knots were.

Ronald would not be pleased that the human had tied him here, but that didn't mean he would spare Willie either. It all depended on how much the *ninj-ki-ra* meant to him. Willie was inclined to think it didn't mean all that much, that Ronald had initiated the ritual for personal reasons rather than the spiritual ones for which the *ninj-ki-ra* was introduced on the home world millennia ago.

Now it was only matter of perhaps half an hour to his final—perhaps fatal—meeting with Ronald. If he was right, it was time to commend his spirit to Zon.

Willie began to chant, as yet uncertain why fate had led him here, tied helplessly to a tree while his nemesis was summoned to kill him. And yet he accepted it, even so. If his death was to be on this day, so be it. His essence would survive, at one with the cosmos, even if his body was destroyed. He prayed for the strength to bear the pain with dignity.

The sonorous chanting echoed through the forest, haunting John Ellis as he searched for Ronald. It was as if Willie were trying to draw Ronald to him now, as if he were eager to die. Ellis shook his head, certain he would never understand these lizards.

As he made his way through the woods, he glanced behind him from time to time. On one such occasion, he craned his neck and then turned to see that he had nearly collided with Ronald's towering, red-clad form.

"Ronald!" he cried.

"You recognized me," the alien said. "You grow more astute every day."

Ellis tried to laugh, but he was too frightened of Ronald. The imposing alien stared at him through his glaring yellow eyes. "I hear the sound of chanting," Ronald said.

"Yeah, I captured him for you. He's tied up back there by the blueberry patch."

"You fool," Ronald hissed.

"What?" Ellis took a step backward, wanting to run away from the threatening reptilian monster. "What's wrong, Ronald?"

"You have destroyed the ritual of *ninj-ki-ra*." Ronald's tongue shot out like a snake's. "You must take me to him at once. I must kill him now, due to your bungling."

Chanting from the *ninj-ki-ra*, Ronald allowed John Ellis to lead him back to Willie.

Willie sensed a presence nearing. At first he thought it was Ronald, but it was too soon—and the creature's intelligence was too rudimentary.

A snorting sound rose from the bushes, which moved as if there was a great bulk passing among them. A moment later, a huge black head emerged. It was the same bear he had befriended earlier.

Willie concentrated with all his mental reserves. He had communicated with the bear earlier, but he must go farther than that now.

Closing his eyes, Willie projected his thoughts toward the wild creature. The beast cocked its huge head, staring at him with its pink tongue lolling out of the side of its jaws. It sensed that Willie was speaking to it, but as yet it didn't know what he wanted.

He tried to actually enter the bear's mind on its own level. There was nothing but darkness at first, but then a glimmer of concern flickered across his consciousness— worry about feeding the young, about the coming winter, about the strange creatures who had invaded the island.

Then he felt a direct mind link with the bear!

Willie thought hard about the twine fastening him to the tree. He imagined Ronald killing him while he was helplessly bound. The bear whined in sympathy.

Certain that the beast understood, Willie made a mental image of it chewing at the twine. He tried to visualize this in every detail. His eyes still closed, he felt something warm on his wrist. He did not dare open his eyes for fear that the bear would lose the mental projection. He continued to think of nothing else but his liberation, feeling the bear's saliva on his scales.

"He's stopped chanting," Ronald said, pausing for a moment.

"Maybe he gave up," offered John Ellis. He didn't like the way Ronald was acting at all. "Maybe he just figures he's gonna die and there's nothing he can do about it by chanting."

Ronald scowled at him, his yellow cat's eyes narrowing. In the dark woods, he had no need of his polarized lenses, but Ellis wished that he would put them back on, even so. Those eyes gave him the creeps.

"This way," he said, suddenly realizing that Ronald was waiting for him to take him to Willie.

They hurried through the stands of birch trees, emerging at last at the edge of the blueberry patch.

"He's right over here." John looked around. He could have sworn the alien was tied to one of the trees right here. But he saw nothing except the serpentine coils of white twine lying on the dead leaves.

"I don't believe it!" Ellis shouted. "How did he—"

He turned to face the angry Ronald, a low growl in the Visitor captain's throat.

Ellis tried to smile. "Well," he said, "at least now you can continue the *ninj-ki-ra*."

Chapter 35

Willie sprinted through the woods, hopping over gnarled tree roots and avoiding open spaces between the trees as much as possible. He had escaped Ronald, but just barely. The cruel alien captain would not be far behind.

Breathing heavily, Willie paused for a moment. Which way should he go? Perhaps it would be wisest—and safest—to plunge into the deepest part of the forest, toward the center of the island. If he was in the middle, he could flee in any direction if Ronald was catching up with him. On the other hand, he couldn't risk going too far and coming out on the narrow beach on the east side of the island, where Ronald's minions were surely patrolling.

For that matter, they were on the west side and the north and south. Willie tried not to despair as he began to run again. He must remember the ordeal of Amon, exiled from the planet of his birth, and take comfort from the Great One's suffering.

He silently repeated the ritual of Zon in his mind as he darted from one clump of trees to another like a creature born to the forest.

The light shone more brightly ahead, suggesting to Willie that there was an open space. He would circle around it, he decided. Curiosity caused him to get a little closer to it, however, and he was surprised by what he saw.

In the clearing were mossy tree stumps and a path leading to a crude dwelling made of timbers.

Though there was a danger in stepping into the clearing, it occurred to Willie that there might be something useful in the cabin, some tool or—Zon forgive him—some weapon. He was ahead of Ronald, so there was little danger that he would get caught in the open if he acted now.

Leaping into the clearing, Willie ran the fifty yards to the cabin. In seconds he was at the door. He tried it but it seemed to be stuck.

He went around to the side. There was clear plastic over the windows. Willie tore it with his claws and punched out the fragile wooden support that made the separate halves of the window too narrow to admit him. There was plenty of room now. He pulled himself up to the casement and perched on the windowsill. After the glaring late afternoon sunlight, it was difficult to see, but it didn't look as though anything would obstruct the leap inside.

But was it worthwhile going in? In the dim light, it wasn't possible to be certain, but Willie could vaguely perceive a few likely objects lying around.

He jumped softly into the room.

Lighting on all fours, Willie kept completely still for a few seconds, the points protruding from his forehead quivering. He knew at once that he had made a mistake. There was someone here.

The old sofa in the corner suddenly lurched forward and toppled over. A bearded man and a young woman were revealed.

"I know what you've come for," the man said.

Willie looked at him, wondering what he meant.

"I've got it right here," the old man told him, seeming to think he would understand. "Come a little closer and I'll give it to you."

Willie remained silent.

The bearded man, emboldened by Willie's reticence, took a step closer. He held up his hand, fingers clenched around something that Willie couldn't see.

"I do not understand," Willie said. "Please explain."

"I can do better than explain," the man replied, a strange gleam in his eye. "I can show you."

Suddenly the man rushed forward, his hand jerking, liquid splashing into Willie's face.

Stepping back, the bearded man opened his hand. A small crystal vial fell to the floor.

At first Willie thought that he had been challenged in some way. He had seen a film once in which wine was thrown into a man's face to force him to fight a duel. But then Willie remembered that such violent customs were a thing of the past on Earth.

He felt a tingling sensation on his face, running down his chest. It was on the inside too, heating his guts, spreading through his veins to the tips of his taloned hands and feet.

The heat increased, flames burning inside him. They threatened to consume him, and yet, even as he was burning up he felt a terrible cold enveloping him.

Trembling from the effects of the icy fire, Willie staggered toward the bearded man.

"What have you done to me?" he said.

"I've killed you," the man replied.

"But I am not your enemy," Willie rasped, guessing now who the bearded man was. "I am running from them too."

"You're one of them," the young woman said.

"One of them," Willie said, "but sent by the resistance to help you."

"Then you're Willie," the woman cried. "You found us."

"Yes," said Willie, "but I fear that others are not far behind me, others who are not sympathetic."

Willie tried to gesture to indicate the direction from which he'd come, but it was no good. He stumbled, his vision fading as the toxin spread through his nervous system. He could barely see the floor coming up to meet him as he fell.

Chapter 36

Dr. Brunk and Sarah Foley stared aghast as Willie lay flopping like a fish out of water on the cabin floor.

"Good Lord," Dr. Brunk shouted. "What have I done?"

He fell to his knees beside Willie and turned the alien over onto his back.

"We still have the antitoxin," Sarah said.

"But we don't know if it will work."

"The toxin seems to be working very well." Sarah reached for the other vials on the table. "So the antitoxin will probably work too."

"The chances are not so great that it will work," Dr. Brunk said. "The cells will be affected very quickly, and the nervous system is already suffering ill effects. Quickly."

Sarah handed him a vial. Dr. Brunk was trying to hold Willie's head up with one hand while he administered the antidote with the other. But Willie's convulsions made it difficult for him.

"Sarah, help me hold him still," Dr. Brunk said. "I can't handle him alone."

As he spoke to her, his face turned away from Willie. At that moment, Willie's convulsions became more violent. He doubled over, arms flailing.

The vial was knocked out of Dr. Brunk's hand, shattering on the stones of the fireplace.

Dr. Brunk shouted, "Another one, Sarah! More antitoxin!"

A terrible rattle started deep in Willie's throat, his neck bulging and a noxious black liquid streaming from his gaping mouth. The rattle increased in frequency and pitch, escalating into a death scream.

Willie's body was vibrating now, wildly out of control. He rolled on the floor, spasming, torso jackknifing in a way that would have broken a human back.

Sarah held the second bottle of the antidote as Dr. Brunk helplessly attempted to restrain the stricken Willie. Brunk was flung against a wall, the breath knocked out of him, his face losing color.

Sarah forgot about Willie, and ran to help her mentor.

Gasping, Dr. Brunk shook his head. "No, I'm all right," he said. "We've got to help him before it's too late."

"Right." Sarah tried to subdue Willie by pulling his arms behind his back, but her fingers slipped on his scales and he thrust her away with ease. She fell on the upended couch, legs askew while Willie writhed, splintering a wooden chair without noticing, flinging himself into the wall, and screaming horribly as he foamed black at the mouth.

"We'd better rush him at the same time." Sarah glanced at Dr. Brunk, and he gave her the thumbs-up signal. "Now."

They both charged at Willie as his clawed hands clutched the empty air, a vase crashing as he collided with the one table still left standing.

One on each arm, they tried to hold him. Willie swung them around as if they were nothing more than rag dolls, annoying bits of flesh to cast away from him in his suffering. They ended up in a tangled heap on the floor, Willie still wailing and howling like a banshee.

"The toxin," Dr. Brunk said through gritted teeth. "Look."

Willy had knocked over the table the vials were on,

and they were scattered over the floor. Dark stains formed where a stopper had come loose, the toxin spilling out, lost forever.

"We've got to save what's left," Sarah cried. She crawled across the floor, picking up the vials. The one that had lost its stopper had just a few drops in it, but the other was completely full of toxin. The one in her hand was the only remaining bottle of the antidote.

Faced with the imminent death of Willie, Sarah decided that she had to take a chance. She pulled the stopper out of the antitoxin vial and ran at Willie, trying to splash it in his face.

Willie slapped her hand away. For a moment she thought he was going to attack her, but then she saw his eyes. There was no anger in them, no hatred. Only sadness and pain.

Willie could not control his body at all, and he was dying. He apparently was unaware of what was happening around him now.

"I never anticipated the violence of the reaction," Dr. Brunk said. "It's all but impossible to administer the antitoxin."

"We can't just let him die," Sarah said. "He came here to help us."

As Willie smashed headfirst into the wall, Dr. Brunk said helplessly, "What can we do?"

Desperate, Sarah looked around at the wreckage of the cabin's interior. The poker clanked onto the floor as Willie gyrated wildly. She darted toward it and scooped it up.

Now Willie was actually climbing up onto the mantel, shrieking horribly with the agony of the virulent serum coursing through his veins. His body stiffened as he tried to stand, he teetered, lost his balance, and landed on the floor with a resounding thud.

Sarah didn't waste any more time. This might kill him, but he was going to die anyway if something wasn't done.

Before Willie could get up off the floor, she brought the poker down hard on the base of his skull.

Chapter 37

"Turn him over," Dr. Brunk said. Together they flipped over his limp form, and Dr. Brunk pulled the powerful, fanged jaws open and poured the last vial of antitoxin down Willie's throat. Somehow Sarah had managed to hang onto it in the fray.

The alien's body was still trembling, the yellow eyes rolled up so that only the daggerlike bottoms of the corneas could be seen. Sarah and Dr. Brunk backed away as the antitoxin worked its way into Willie's system—for good or ill.

Low moans escaped Willie's gurgling throat. His jaws opened wide, hinges working to reveal a maw three times the size of a human's.

"If the antitoxin comes back up," Dr. Brunk said, "the residue might not be enough to save him."

"We've done what we could," Sarah breathed. "There's no more antitoxin."

Willie's convulsions seemed milder now. Was it the lull before the final storm, or was the antitoxin taking effect? They could only wait and see.

In a way, though neither of them would admit it, it was a relief for Dr. Brunk and Sarah. The toxin had been tested, and it worked very well, obviously. They did not know this Visitor, and the challenge of having to accept him after testing him with the toxin disturbed them. Both of them knew that these feelings were not humanistic, and yet neither of them could help themselves. They had spent months learning to hate the Visitors, and though they welcomed Willie to their cause, they feared they would never be comfortable with the alien.

On the other hand, neither of them wanted him to die. They could assure themselves that they had tried to save him. Now, if he pulled through, there was the possibility of the camaraderie—the *esprit de corps*—of the New England resistance being shattered. Things become too complicated when the lizards began to work with humans against their own. There was no doubt human kind needed Willie and others like him, but now that his usefulness had ended, what would they do with him? It wasn't that they didn't consider him the equal of a human being. Indeed, that was the problem; Willie might be more than equal to a human.

Willie was still now, a pool of the black bile beside his head. They waited for him to show some sign of life.

After a few minutes, Sarah said, "Do you think he's alive?"

"I don't know," Dr. Brunk said. "I don't know what vital signs these organisms might show. When that prisoner was in our laboratory, it was all guesswork, and he was gone before we learned very much."

"Only enough to kill them," Sarah whispered.

"That is often one of the first things we learn about an organism," observed Dr. Brunk. "It's a strange thing, that."

They fell silent, grappling internally with the mysteries of life and death as this living being hovered on the brink before their eyes. Dr. Brunk considered that it was truly a test of their commitment, to see the effects of the new viral toxin first in actual field conditions, rather than in the laboratory.

Willie stirred, disturbing Brunk's reverie. Hawklike, the scientist's eyes watched the stricken Visitor intently. Willie's head turned slowly toward them, his eyes in focus and clearing recognizing his surroundings.

"Dr. Brunk," he said weakly. "I thought I was going to die."

"Don't talk now. Sarah, help me turn that sofa back upright. He needs to get some rest."

A moment later, they were stooping to help Willie onto the sofa. His lean muscles were soft and pliable now beneath his scaly skin, not stiff and unyielding as they had been in Willie's sick frenzy.

"Forgive my violence," Willie said. "I was not my own master for a vile."

"A vile?" Sarah questioned.

"I mean 'a while.' I was stationed in Saudi Arabia when I first came to Earth, and I have never learned the English hexacon very well."

"I think you mean 'lexicon,' but it doesn't matter right now," Sarah said. "Can I get you something, Willie?"

"Water."

"I'll get some for you." She started toward the door.

"Do you think you should go outside now?" Dr. Brunk said. "It might not be safe."

"I'll be all right." She unbolted the door and went out into the cool air. The sun was going down now, the shadows of the pines very long. Sarah walked to the pump behind the cabin and realized that she had forgotten to bring a container for the water.

Starting back toward the cabin, she began to feel guilty about her feelings toward Willie when he appeared to be dying. She was starting to like him already, after only a few words of conversation.

Almost to the door now, she heard something behind her. She hesitated and then turned. Coming out of the shadowy forest was a creature who looked like Willie, wearing a crimson uniform.

She ran the rest of the way.

Chapter 38

Dr. Brunk and Willie looked up in surprise as Sarah slammed and bolted the cabin door.

"They're out there," she said breathlessly.

Dr. Brunk shook his head. "All we have left is this one vial of toxin," he said. "If we pour it out, they get nothing but the satisfaction of killing us."

"They will try to convert you," Willie said. "To fry the formula out of you."

"It won't work." Dr. Brunk smiled bitterly. "My heart would never hold up under conversion. I'll take the formula to the grave with me."

"Don't be so certain," Willie advised. "They have ways that are more subtle than you might think."

"I suppose that's true, but I may not be able to remember enough of the formula, and my notes have been destroyed, Willie."

"Please assist me to my feet," Willie said. "I must be prepared to meet Ronald."

"Ronald . . . is he their leader?"

"Yes, he commands a squadron," Willie said. "Working with a human in the village, he has managed to kill many of the young males. There is little left of the local resistance now, or at least Ronald boasts that this is so."

"Did he follow you here?"

"Yes, he made me the quarry in an ancient ritual, the *ninj-ki-ra*, knowing that my trail must lead ultimately to you . . . and to the toxin."

"Well, it seems to have worked," Sarah put in. "I wonder what they're doing out there."

"Congratulating themselves, most likely," said Dr. Brunk. "It looks as if they've won."

"They cannot win if you do not permit them to," Willie said. "Ronald fears the truth, for there is strength in it that he will never know. You must remember that, for he will try to rob you of your strength and thus rob you of the truth."

"I don't know what the truth is, Willie," Dr. Brunk said softly, astonished at how deeply this alien moved him. "I'm fighting for the life of my people, my world."

"There is great truth in that," Willie said, "perhaps more than we can know by ourselves, but comprehended by the universe itself, the greatest of all entities, of which we are all a part."

"How can such warlike people have such profound beliefs?" Sarah asked.

"We are complex, just like you."

"Willie," Dr. Brunk said, "I must tell you that I didn't really want you to live a few minutes ago, but I'm glad you did."

"You have glimpsed some small glimmer of the universal truth, then?"

Dr. Brunk smiled. "Perhaps."

A searing blue bolt shot through the open window, burning a hole through the opposite wall. Sarah recoiled in terror, the beam missing her by inches.

"Ronald," Willie called out as he made his way painfully to the window, "You have won. I'm coming out."

There was no reply.

"You have tracked me down," Willie said. "There is no place left for me to run. My life is yours to end, according to the *ninj-ki-ra*."

Silence.

Willie turned to the Sarah and Dr. Brunk. "He waits for me to tell what else there is for him here."

"Don't submit to him, Willie," Dr. Brunk said. "You can't save us."

"I must try."

Dr. Brunk held up his right hand. In it was the last of the vials, a gleaming thing that was one of the few hopes the human race had now.

"Dr. Brunk," said Sarah, "I'm going to build a fire."

"Why?" Willie asked.

"He can pour the contents of that last bottle into the flames, and there'll be no trace of the toxin or the antidote left. That's the best thing we can do now."

She began to stuff old newspapers into the fireplace, tossing some split logs in and lighting a match to ignite it.

"You cannot destroy it," Willie said. "It is your only hope."

"We can't let them have it, Willie."

"You don't know what will happen," Willie said. "And this young woman may need something to protect her."

Dr. Brunk had started toward the fire, but now he stopped and stared at Willie. "What are you saying?"

"You have not heard of . . . atrocities?"

Now Willie had Sarah's attention too.

"What would they want with me?" she asked.

"There is much about my people you do not understand," Willie said. "Ancient beliefs about mammalian creatures much like yourselves. Sick desires among some of us to humiliate, torment, destroy."

Sarah and Dr. Brunk looked terrified. They glanced at one another meaningfully.

"Keep the last vial," Dr. Brunk said. "Hide it on your person, Sarah, in case you need it."

Sarah nodded. "Okay." She slipped the vial into the hip pocket of her jeans.

At that moment, the cabin door was blasted off its hinges.

Chapter 39

A towering figure stood framed in the doorway, the dying daylight piercing the smoke curling around him.

"Ronald," Willie said. "You have come for me at last."

"I have come for more than you, my little philosopher," Ronald grated. "But you have not told me what else is here for me, as you must according to the *ninj-ki-ra*."

"There is nothing for you here, only my soul, which you will set free."

"You lie!" Ronald hissed. Dr. Brunk and Sarah shrank at the terrible sound, but Willie appeared unafraid. He stood his ground as Ronald entered the smoky room.

"You know the truth, then?" Willie asked.

"Ah, you moralistic disciples of Amon think you and you alone possess the virtue of truth. I am here to tell you that there are many truths, and there are no truths."

"This seems a conundrum," said Willie.

"Too complex for your simple minded religiosity?" Ronald sneered. "No doubt you are trying to convince yourself that what I have said is mere doggerel, but somewhere inside you is the certainty that the universe is not merely two-dimensional, as your faith insists. We would all be much happier if it were true, no doubt, but we would not be as we are."

"You know some of the truth," Willie said.

"Then you have no argument before we begin the final act of this little drama?"

"Only that you lie to yourself even as you speak the truth."

Ronald hissed and then beckoned to those outside to surround the cabin. Willie could see them through the open door and the window, fifteen or twenty soldiers, the red of their uniforms standing out starkly against the earthen colors of the forest. They surrounded the cabin in a matter of seconds. There was no way out.

"The *ninj-ki-ra* demands a quick end," Willie said.

"There are complications that render the precepts of the *ninj-ki-ra* somewhat inadequate to this situation," Ronald said. "Specifically, the presence of Dr. Brunk and his assistant."

"Let them go," Willie said.

"If the formula is turned over to me, I may consider that option," Ronald said, his wicked amber eyes turning to Dr. Brunk.

"There is no formula," Dr. Brunk told him. "It's been destroyed."

"Then you will simply give me the toxin—and the antidote."

"All gone." Dr. Brunk pointed at the rough, wooden floor, "There is the last of it, seeping into those boards."

Ronald clucked. "Then we will extract the formula from your brain, Dr. Brunk."

Sarah had moved close to Dr. Brunk in a protective way. He felt her shuddering against him now. This was what she had feared.

"Do what you will, Ronald. There is no way you will learn how to cook that toxin. Your hunt has been in vain."

"Nonsense." Ronald's neck ballooned in annoyance. "You did not flee to this island because you had nothing to hide. Now turn the toxin over to me before I lose my patience.''

Taking heart from Willie's courageous example, the doctor faced Ronald squarely and shook his head. He knew that he had just signed his own death warrant, but he wasn't as frightened as he had always thought he would be when his time came. Indeed, he took a certain satisfaction in knowing that he had done everything he could to fight the Visitors. Someone else would develop the toxin, even if he died. At least he would not give it to them of his own free will. "I won't," he said. "I can't."

"Very well," Ronald said. "You have chosen the role of hero in our little drama, Dr. Brunk. It becomes you, I suppose, the noble man of science defying the evil invader to the last. Tedious, but admirable." He turned and beckoned at someone outside the door.

Two soldiers entered and then a man whom Dr. Brunk didn't recognize. Sarah knew him, though. She had known him all her life, and feared him.

It was John Ellis.

"Unlike some of my people," Ronald said, "I have no interest in your species other than a problematical one—and, of course, a culinary one. No, sex is something I enjoy with members of my own species only. Most—but not all—humans seem to feel the same way. The striking thing about human sexuality, at least in my limited observation, is how selective the female can be, considering that males are outnumbered.

"Young woman, what do you think of this specimen of manhood?" He indicated Ellis with a clawed hand.

Sarah said nothing.

"Ah, perhaps reticence means something, but what?" Ronald sighed. "I know so little about human custom. It strikes me, however, that the demure female is pleased that we have brought John Ellis here. Or am I mistaken?''

"You're very mistaken," Sarah said angrily.

"Oh, then you are among the choosy ones. Excellent, excellent." Ronald's neck swelled with pleasure. "Then it should make your mating all the more interesting."

Chapter 40

John Ellis lumbered toward Sarah, a crooked, leering grin on his red face. It occurred to Willie that Ronald had learned much more about human sexuality than he admitted. How else could he have arranged such a perverse confrontation? He had not educated himself in the ways of humans for intellectual reasons, clearly. Every fact he acquired had but one rationale: to defeat and demoralize the enemy.

The look of horror on Sarah's face could not have been more intense if Ronald himself were about to assault her.

"Stay away from her!" Dr. Brunk shouted. "Can't you see she doesn't want anything to do with you?"

"Shut up, you old fool," snarled Ellis.

"Yes, do be quiet, Dr. Brunk," Ronald said. "This is far too edifying a spectacle for you to spoil with your blathering."

Ellis' beefy hand shot out with surprising speed and caught Sarah's wrist. He pulled her roughly toward him.

Instead of fear, Sarah's face showed indignation and anger. As her body collided with her attacker's, her knee came up and caught him squarely in the groin.

Ellis grunted. Then he wheezed, sagging to the floor like a slashed tire.

Released, Sarah backed away from the fallen Ellis. "You got off easy this time, sucker," she said.

Ellis slowly got back on his feet. "You bitch."

Ronald clucked appreciatively. Such an unexpected turn of events delighted him, appealing to the same cruel

playfulness that had moved him to include Jake and
Charlie in the equation. He enjoyed surprises, as long as
he controlled the events that produced them.

Sarah shook her pretty head to get the hair out of her
eyes. At that moment, John Ellis charged her like a
roaring bull.

Sarah was taken off guard, tackled like a football
player carrying the ball. Ellis was on top of her on the
floor, trying to tear her clothes open. She pummeled him
with her balled fists, screaming at him to get off her,
trying to use her knees to dislodge him. He had her at a
disadvantage now, her efforts ineffectual against his far
greater bulk. She raked at his face with her nails, and
Ellis bellowed in pain as she drew blood. His head
snapped back, and Sarah somehow wriggled out from
under him.

"She seems to be too much for him," Ronald
observed. "But he doesn't give in easily."

Ellis rolled over and leaped to his feet. This time he
didn't tackle her. Instead, he lunged and punched her
with a meaty fist.

Sarah's head snapped back, and she pirouetted and
collided with a chair lying on its side. She fell backward,
hitting her head on the hardwood floor.

Ellis was on her in an instant. Dazed, Sarah could no
longer struggle as he prepared to have his way with her.
She moaned in half-conscious pain.

"No!" Dr. Brunk cried. He broke free from the guard
holding his arm and pulled Ellis off Sarah. "Let her go,
you animal!"

"Subdue him!" Ronald commanded.

The two soldiers grabbed Dr. Brunk, one on each arm.
He somehow found the strength to shake them off,
lunging at Ronald.

"You monster!" he screamed.

Ronald stood completely still as Brunk attacked him.

He didn't move, even when the doctor collided with him headfirst. Butted in the diaphragm, Ronald looked down at the flailing man with a mocking stare.

All stood in horrified anticipation for a moment, but Ronald did nothing for a few seconds. He waited as Dr. Brunk spent himself on a futile effort at hurting him. Soon the doctor could barely lift his hands to strike. It was then that Ronald acted.

Reaching down, he clutched Dr. Brunk's throat in a viselike grip. Sarah tried to go to him, but the guards stopped her.

Willie watched, saddened but knowing that Randall Brunk had made his choice. This way, Ronald would never learn the formula for the new toxin.

Ronald was thinking only of killing Dr. Brunk. His ostensible purpose for coming to the island was forgotten in his blood lust.

Ronald lifted Dr. Brunk off the floor by the throat. A hacking, gurgling sound escaped Brunk's mouth, flecks of foam falling onto his beard. He dangled face to face with Ronald, and then he was lifted even higher, Ronald staring up at him as he gasped his last.

A snapping sound announced Dr. Brunk's death, the vertebrae in his neck breaking.

Willie chanted silently to himself, honoring the dead man and praying for his soul. Dr. Brunk was at one with the cosmos now, a being who had died with dignity and courage, his essence sent out to enrich the stars.

Ronald suddenly seemed aware of what he had done. He stared in rage at the corpse in his hand and flung Dr. Brunk's body away from him as though the dead man had at last harmed him.

Chapter 41

Ronald's neck ballooned and his scales turned a green so deep that he appeared almost black. He averted his eyes from the broken body of Dr. Brunk on the floor, turning to Willie.

"There is the truth," Willie said, "lying dead on the floor."

"He was a fool!" Ronald bellowed. "An utter fool!"

"That fool has beaten you," Willie told him softly.

"Beaten me? I killed him as easily as I would squash an insect."

"An insect who held a secret you desperately wanted," Willie reminded him.

Ronald's neck bulged with anger, his eyes fiery. He knew that Willie was telling him the truth now. There could be no ambiguity here. He had allowed his rage to defeat him, tricked by a puny human into botching his mission. The traitor stood before him, excoriating him for what he had done, smug, satisfied. This Ronald would not tolerate.

"You," he said to John Ellis.

Ellis, still stunned by Dr. Brunk's valiant death, at first didn't realize Ronald was addressing him.

"Go," Ronald commanded him.

"Go?" Ellis pointed his finger at his own chest. "But I haven't . . ."

"You have done enough. What follows is not for your eyes."

"But you promised me the girl!"

"I promised you nothing. You have never understood power, John Ellis, though you are capable of wielding it in a limited fashion."

"I had twenty-five men following me at one time."

"And you betrayed them," Ronald said. "They trusted you, and you betrayed them. Now what do you have?"

Ellis glanced wildly around the room. "He promised me!" he screamed. "He said if I led those men to him he'd make me a powerful man once the Visitors took over for good."

Sarah's face clearly showed her revulsion.

"And he said—he said if I led him to the mayor, he'd give me—" He gazed imploringly at Sarah. "—he said he'd give me you."

He seemed to shrink under her icy gaze, a man who had squandered his talents on vicious dreams of power. He pointed at Willie.

"He's no better than me!" he shrieked. "Look at him! He's a traitor to his people too!"

"There's a difference," Sarah said.

"A difference? What difference?"

"Willie came over to our side as an act of conscience. You did it out of pure greed."

The desperation in John Ellis' eyes was pathetic. He knew now that Ronald had only used him, that his hatred and resentment had been like blinders. It had been so simple for the alien to manipulate him. Now he felt nothing but shame.

"I'm sorry," he whispered.

But he could see from the expression on Sarah Foley's face that it was too late. The game was over for him. His head dropped onto his chest in abject misery.

"Enough breast beating," Ronald said. "Go now."

Ellis felt the blood pounding through his head. He crouched low as he made his way past Willie, Sarah, and Ronald. And then he bolted through the open doorway.

"Another miscalculation on my part," Ronald said. "Though he served his purpose well enough for a time."

"Pity him," Willie said, "if you know such an emotion Ronald."

"I have heard of it," Ronald responded dryly. "But I admit I have little use for it."

Willie went to Sarah and put his arm around her shoulder. "Did he hurt you?" he asked.

"Not very much. I never knew he was such a frightened little man. I do feel sorry for him, Willie."

"It is good that you feel compassion for him, for he is sick in heart and spirit."

"Spare me," Ronald said. "You think you've won, and perhaps you have. Somehow, though, I don't believe it. It seems to me that there might yet be living someone who has knowledge of that elusive toxin."

Willie felt Sarah's trembling.

"No," Willie said. "You heard him say that even he could not reconstruct the formula easily."

"It would have come back to him, given the proper incentives, and it might yet be possible to obtain the formula."

"You're dreaming."

"Yes, and my dreams are quite vivid, Willie. As are yours."

Ronald came toward them, a powerful, looming figure, his frontal ridges protruding like the horns of a demon.

"Our methods must be crude, unfortunately," he

rasped, "for the time is short before we board the skyfighter."

"The skyfighter? Why?"

"We will use it to attack the village. There must be no survivors to tell that we have acquired the new toxin."

Chapter 42

"But there is no reason to kill the people in Cutter's Cove," Willie said. "The formula is no more."

"I suspect that is not entirely true," Ronald observed.

"But what good will it do to slaughter them?" Sarah cried. "If you get the toxin, the resistance will figure out why you killed them."

"Not if we convert a survivor to tell them that we did not find it. That they still have a weapon to use against us. We will have taken another step toward the complete subjugation of your planet."

"And if you don't get the toxin?"

"Then humankind will have another reason to fear us."

"So you're going to wipe out Cutter's Cove no matter what," Sarah said. She thought of her mother waiting for her to come home, alone in that big old house. "You're going to kill them all."

"It would seem the expedient thing to do."

"My God." Sarah broke down and wept, a human habit during stress that Willie found curiously moving.

"How can you be so heartless?" she sniffled. "How can you and Willie be so different?"

"He is not bred for war, as I am," Ronald said matter-of-factly. "I had little say in becoming what I am."

"But you have a free will. How can you do such monstrous things?"

"It is for the best," Ronald said. "For my people,

there is not enough water and protein. The conquest of Earth will solve that problem, at least for a while.''

"Why can't you just change your ways? Do you really need to rape our world for your needs? Why didn't you ask us to help you?''

Was that an ironic gleam she spotted in Ronald's eye? "We observed much about your planet before we came here," he said. "Kindness toward strangers seemed a rather rare commodity here, even before we came.''

Sarah shook her head. It was no use arguing with him; he had an answer for everything. There were many different forms of truth, as Ronald had said, and his was not the same as the truth she knew.

"Enough of this pointless discussion," Ronald said. "I have something for you, young woman, something to refresh your memory.''

Ronald's left claw reached under his protective vest and withdrew a pointed device.

"No!" Willie cried. He tried to move toward Ronald to stop him, but he was restrained by the guards.

Ronald squeezed the device and a green wave emerged from its tip. The wave seemed to bend the light that passed through it, distorting what could be seen through it.

Sarah was enveloped in the light, wrapped in an emerald cocoon. For a moment, she didn't seem to realize what had happened, but then her eyes opened wide.

She screamed in pain as her central nervous system was charged with a burning energy field. Willie watched in helpless horror as she writhed within the field, unable to escape its powerful hold.

Ronald wielded the pain wand for over a minute before he allowed Sarah a respite. Suddenly the green light vanished, and she sank to the floor, shaking from head to toe.

"Please," Willie said. "Such a primitive use of physical pain is unwarranted."

"Is it?" Ronald said. But the question was rhetorical, Willie saw as the cruel Visitor captain once again turned the wand on Sarah.

"For the sake of Amon," Willie cried. "Please stop. Have you not seen enough suffering, Ronald?"

"Perhaps," Ronald said, "she will reconsider the possibility that the formula remains extant even after the death of Dr. Brunk."

Sarah's screams smothered much of what Ronald said, but his meaning was clear. He inflicted pain coolly and efficiently, as if he had done it many times before. Indeed, he seemed to enjoy his work.

"Turn it off," Willie said. "She will talk."

"Do you think so?" Ronald fired one last jolt at Sarah and then shut off the wand again.

Sarah was turned faceup, her back arched, mouth opened wide in a silent scream. Her body collapsed like a puppet whose strings had been severed. She lay gasping on the floor as Ronald stood over her.

"The formula," he said. "Where is it?"

"I don't know," Sarah moaned.

"You irk me," Ronald said. "Both of you. But you, Willie, will have to wait for your reward."

Ronald applied the wand again, this time increasing its intensity. The emerald field brightened, a long, tortured wail emerging from the obscured image of Sarah within it.

"You have already killed the man who could have helped you, and you got nothing out of him," Willie said. "Will you also kill the girl?"

Ronald distractedly tormented Sarah for a few more seconds, and then he shut off the wand again.

"You are quite correct, Willie," he said. "You are a remarkable fellow, you know." He showed his fangs.

"The young woman seems to have grown quite fond of you. Let us see how she reacts to the sight of you being tortured."

The tip of the wand glowed, throwing a glittering emerald web over Willie before he could even speak.

Chapter 43

Willie told himself at the deepest level he could reach that the pain was not intolerable. This he had learned from the *preta-na-ma*. It remained a great challenge, a challenge he had forgotten when the toxin was thrown in his face.

A million needles pierced him, green and crackling with sinister energy. He willed himself to feel nothing. For a moment all sensations were blotted out. But they slowly emerged. Like water seeping through a crack under a door, they spilled into his consciousness: the sparkling emerald field, the low humming sound, the odor and taste of ozone—and the agony as his nervous system was savaged.

Redoubling his effort to fight the pain, Willie pushed his senses back under the door of his perception. But he was so weak from his earlier ordeal that he could barely remain conscious. He felt his energy draining away from him, the pain seeping through again—more of it than before. The door threatened to brust from the pressure on the other side. . . .

Somewhere beyond the hum, he heard Sarah scream.

Walking slowly through the woods, his gun left behind at the cabin, John Ellis wondered what would become of him now. He couldn't go back home. He couldn't face his neighbors, not after this. How could he have done such terrible things? All those people dead, and for what? Ronald had never intended to give him any power.

What a fool he had been. Ronald wouldn't let him go home now anyway. He knew too much. The only reason the lizard hadn't killed him back there, John supposed, was that he was too preoccupied with getting the formula, not to mention torturing Willie and Sarah.

All the guards were back at the cabin. If he knew how to fly the skyfighter, he'd take it and get the hell out of the state of Maine altogether. That was out of the question, though. But there was the boat Brunk and Sarah had rowed out here. It was only a little over a mile to the mainland. He could do it before they noticed he was gone. He'd go home, get a bus out of town, go to Portland or Hartford or even Boston. Nobody around here would ever see him again.

He heard a rustling in the bushes.

Maybe he hadn't counted all the guards at the cabin. Could he have missed one? The way he was thrashing around in the bushes, John doubted it.

It was probably those two New Yorkers. Of course. He could hear them talking now, "dese" and "dose" New Yorkese clearly audible. Some hunters—they would scare away any game that came within a mile of them.

John waded into the bushes, thinking that he would take their guns. That way, if he ran into any trouble with lizard guards along the way, he could shoot first.

The last of the bushes crunched underfoot as he emerged into a tiny clearing. There they were, looking the wrong way, wondering what was making all the noise and where it was coming from.

"Over here, boys," said John Ellis.

Jake and Charlie turned around, fear etched in their faces. Before they could see who it was, Charlie's gun went off.

It was pointed directly at Ellis' chest.

* * *

The recoil nearly knocked Charlie down. The rifle had been down at his hip, and the butt had bruised him badly, but he was still standing.

John Ellis wasn't. He had been blown back into the bushes as the bullet passed through his chest. Charlie hadn't realized the safety was off. He stared down at it now in disbelief. Smoke curled from the barrel.

"I shot him," he murmured.

"Yeah," Jake agreed, "you sure did."

"Christ, I killed him."

"Looks like it, but you've got to admit the bastard had it coming."

"Maybe so," Charlie said, his eyes widening, "but he was Ronald's main man. You think that lizard is gonna like it?"

"He'll get over it," Jake said uncertainly. "It was an accident."

"It won't be any accident when he gets his hands on me," Jake opined.

"Well, maybe we can hide the body."

"Right. Or feed it to the bear." Jake began to take heart. "If we feed him to the bear, Ronald will never suspect we had anything to do with it."

"Let's pull him out of those bushes and drag him over to the blueberry patch," Charlie said. "The bear's sure to find him over there."

They stepped clumsily into the bushes, cracking the branches underfoot as they labored to free Ellis' body. The shot had passed through him cleanly, so they didn't have to contend with much blood as long as they pulled him by his arms and legs.

Breathing heavily, they managed to get him out onto the leaf-strewn clearing.

A voice said: "Hold it right there."

They looked up into the barrel of a shotgun.

Chapter 44

Pythias Day looked down the sight of his scatter-gun at two men dragging a dead body.

"Looks like you fellows have got some explaining to do," he said.

"He was our guide," Charlie said, trying to explain.

"Was that any reason to shoot him?" Pythias demanded.

"No, of course not. It was an accident. He turned us over to the Visitors, and—"

"That's John Ellis," a woman's voice noted. Jane Foley stepped out of from behind a tree, a pistol in her dainty hand. "They've done the world a favor."

"I thought he was that bear," Charlie said. "I didn't know it was— What did you say?"

"I said you've done the world a favor. This man was a traitor."

"Yes, he was. How did you know?"

"It's a long story," said Jane. She whistled, and suddenly people started to come out of the woods. They were all armed, some only with knives, one or two with tools and farming implements, but most had guns. That wasn't their most striking feature, however. There were only a handful of men, and the rest were women and youngsters.

"I'll be damned," said Jake.

"We might not have the weapons the Visitors have," Pythias said, "but we've got them outnumbered."

"How did you get on the island with all those lizards crawling around?" Jake asked.

"We kept a close watch on the place, cruising by the nearest islands and keeping out of sight. A little while ago they all abandoned the beach and went toward the interior of the island. We think we know why."

Jake and Charlie glanced at each other. "We're free," Jake said.

"That's right," Pythias told them. "You can wait it out while we go after them—or you can join us."

They both nodded. "We're with you," said Jake. "This planet belongs to all of us, so I guess that makes it our fight as much as yours."

Pythias flashed one of his rare grins. "Welcome aboard."

"What do we do to help?" Charlie wanted to know.

"Somewhere on this island there's an old cabin. A doctor who's developed a toxin to fight the Visitors is hiding there. He has a young woman with him, his assistant. They went there because the place is secluded, hard to find. A good idea, until the Visitors caught up with them."

"So we have to find the cabin and make like the Lone Ranger, is that it?" The prospect seemed to please Jake. "What are we waiting for?"

They fanned out, a search party nearly forty strong. Pythias and Jane went together, both of them praying that Sarah was still alive.

Willie dropped to the floor, retching and quaking violently. He could no longer fight the pain; he was simply too weak for such an intense concentration. Ronald had been torturing him for what seemed an eternity, playing with him as a cat plays with a mouse.

"For God's sake!" Sarah screamed. "Stop it!"

"God?" Ronald mused. "What god? Yours or Willie's?" He gave Willie another jolt with the wand, lifting him to his feet against his will.

Willie's tongue snaked out of his mouth involuntarily, flecks of foam dripping from it. Ronald moved the wand slowly from left to right, forcing Willie to shamble in a grotesque parody of a dance. His body twisted into positions no human being had ever seen before, and Sarah couldn't take it anymore.

"Please," she said. "If you stop it, I'll give you what you want."

The green light was switched off, and Willie collapsed once again.

"I knew you could be reasonable," Ronald said, "given the proper incentive."

"Thank you," Willie gasped from the floor, "but you shouldn't have capitulated."

"I couldn't let him kill you," Sarah said. She tried to go to him, but the guard restrained her.

"Let her go," Ronald commanded.

Sarah knelt and gently placed Willie's head on her lap. "Are you all right?" she asked tenderly.

"Yes, I will recover, but you should have let him kill me."

"I couldn't let you sacrifice your life, not after the courage you've shown."

"How maudlin," Ronald sneered. "Enough of these histrionics. Where is the formula?"

"It's not here," said Sarah.

"Where, then?"

"On the mainland," she lied, "at my home."

Ronald took a step forward, looming over Sarah and Willie.

"If you are lying—and we shall soon know if you are, for my soldiers await my orders to assemble for the final attack on your village—if I find that you are lying, it will go very badly for you."

"It's the truth." She had to stall for time, and it was the only thing she could think of.

Ronald's claw grasped her wrist, dragging her to her feet. Willie propped himself up on one elbow, trying to get onto his feet, but it was no good. He fell back onto the floor.

Ronald turned toward the door. At that moment, one of his soldiers appeared in the empty door frame, speaking wildly in the alien tongue.

Before Ronald could answer him, a gunshot rang out and the soldier clutched his head, falling across the threshold dead.

Chapter 45

Gunshots and laser fire filled the autumn air around the cabin. Ronald backed away from the door, confused for the first time since he had come to Earth.

"The resistance," Sarah cried, trying to break free of Ronald's grip.

He was far too strong for her as he gestured for guards to go out and join the fray. One of them didn't make it past the corpse on the floor; he was hit by a laser bolt and collapsed, limbs entwined with his late comrade-in-arms.

Shots echoed thunderously through the forest as the resistance fighters fired from the shelter of the trees. Only the rifle reports gave the Visitors something to shoot at, but even this was misleading, the resistance fighters quickly scurrying from one tree to another while the red-garbed Visitors presented wonderful targets.

At the last someone came out of the trees. The nearest of the Visitors squinted at what appeared to be gleaming body armor of some kind. He fired his laser.

The beam struck the gleaming figure and bounced back, bending so that it shot harmlessly into the trees, burning off a bough in a shower of cinders. The resistance fighter held a full-length mirror, the perfect defensive weapon against a laser.

It was extremely difficult to wound a Visitor while he wore his protective vest, as Pythias had discovered to his chagrin a few days before at the laboratory. He had warned Jane, Herb Walsh, Mike Sherman, and the others to go for the head or try to shoot the leg out from under them. Otherwise, they were just wasting ammunition.

The Visitors were in disarray, their leader sequested inside the cabin. Without orders, they darted aimlessly back and forth, sometimes nearly colliding as they searched for targets. The clearing filled with smoke and the odor of burned gunpowder as the Visitors were picked off one at a time.

Pythias had personally dispatched two of them, the best shooting he'd done since enlisting in the Army at twenty-seven, back in the Second World War. It was easy with the laser pistol, the enemy out front like sitting ducks.

Six or seven of them went down before the Visitors ever knew what hit them. Clumped together in front of the cabin, blinded by the dying sunlight in their faces, three more fell in a matter of seconds.

The remaining five scattered, gibbering at each other in their own language as they dodged a hail of bullets.

Peg MacGregor hit one of them in the leg. He fell to the ground moaning, and she pumped three more shots into him. At that moment, Don Curtis led a Visitor in his sights, squeezing off a shot the alien walked right into. Mrs. Snodgrass, enjoying her first day off in twenty-two years, happily blasted away with her late husband's 30-30. Arvid Ebbeson did his best to redeem himself, carefully selecting his shots.

But it was Herb Walsh who brought down the last of the alien fighting force with a single shot from his old German Mauser.

"All right," Pythias said. "That only leaves Ronald."

Jane glanced at him, barely daring to hope that her daughter was in that cabin, alive and whole.

"Come on out of there," Pythias shouted. "It's over!"

Ronald hissed his fury at the sound of Pythias Day's voice. How could that aging, hairy simian have done this to him? He drew his laser pistol from its holster, still clutching Sarah's wrist.

"It is true," Willie said weakly from the floor. "It is over, just as Pythias Day has said."

Snarling, Ronald leveled the laser at Willie's head. "You will not live to see his victory."

"No!" Sarah struck his wrist, deflecting the blue energy bolt. It burned off the leg of a table standing on its side. The table leg clunked onto the floor and rolled next to Willie, who opened his mouth as if to speak.

He began to chant from the ritual of Zon.

"Silence!" Ronald commanded.

Willie obediently stopped chanting, which infuriated Ronald even more. The sound of his grating teeth was audible, and his neck swelled out in agitation. "Why have I been cursed with you, Willie?" he roared.

"You have always been victorious in the past, Ronald," said Willie, "and so you thought it was your due to always win. But it is not. You have lost, and so it is best you surrender gracefully."

Pythias Day's voice rose from the forest. "If you come out now, we'll do what we can for the wounded. But we can't be responsible for them, if you stay in there. If we step into the open to help them, you might shoot at us."

Growling, Ronald fired a series of blue beams into the forest.

"Is that your answer?" Willie said. "To let the soldiers who have served you die? To sacrifice them because your pride has been damaged?"

Ronald's forked tongue flickered in and out of his jaws as he considered his dilemma.

He turned to Willie at length and said with satisfaction, "There is still the skyfighter."

Chapter 46

"Get him to his feet," Ronald commanded.

"He's too weak," Sarah protested.

"If he is not on his feet in five seconds, I will kill him." Ronald released her wrist.

Sarah stooped to help Willie up. He slowly got to his feet and stood, weak but unbowed, facing Ronald. "Do with me what you will," he said.

"Why won't you fight?" Ronald demanded angrily. "I know you have courage. Why do you not want to kill me, even now?"

"I cannot harm you," Willie said. "You are dead inside. The living cannot harm the dead."

"Perhaps not," Ronald said, pulling Sarah toward him once again. "But the dead can hurt the living, it seems."

"What do you want with her now?" Willie asked.

"She is coming with me, and so are you."

Willie nodded, understanding that the *ninj-ki-ra* was, in a sense, not over yet. He leaned against the wall for support as he waited for this final stage of the game to begin.

"You go first," Ronald instructed him. "And we follow."

Willie stumbled toward the door, Ronald pushing him forward roughly. A shot rang out, and a piece of the doorjamb turned to splinters and sawdust next to Willie's head.

"Hold your fire!" Pythias Day shouted from cover.

"That's Willie. Besides that, Arvid, we told them they could come out. Now, don't get trigger-happy."

Willie was grateful that the sun was going down as he stepped outside. He nearly fell but somehow kept his balance. Next came Sarah, Ronald's clawed hand around her neck. The laser pistol was held against her right temple.

"Sarah!" Jane Foley cried. She started forward, but Pythias held her back.

"Wait," he whispered.

Ronald did not look at the dying soldiers lying in their own blood. He stared balefully into the forest instead.

"Come out," he said. "All of you, come out or I will kill the woman."

There was no sign that anyone heard him for a moment. Had Ronald miscalculated? Would they risk letting him kill her? In a way, Sarah hoped that they would. But, then, he might not be bluffing.

"Let's do as he says," Pythias called to the resistance fighters.

Slowly they emerged from the forest, women and children mostly, and a few drunks. They were sober enough today, however, given a chance to defend their homes against the invader. Their capitulation to Ronald's demands was resentful, but they couldn't let him kill Sarah. They had all—with the exception of Jake and Charlie—known her all their lives.

They gathered in front of the cabin, rifles pointed down at the ground.

"We are going to leave now," Ronald said. "Willie will go first, and the woman will follow. If anyone attempts to follow, she will die when I am safely away from here."

"My baby!" Jane cried. She tried to come closer, but Ronald shook his squamous head to warn her away.

"Stay where you are," he said.

"Let her go," Pythias Day said, running his hand through his flowing beard, "and we'll let you go."

"You'll let me go without her?" Ronald sneered. "I doubt that. But I know you will let me go if she is with me. Do you think I'm such a fool, Pythias Day?"

"Judging from the mess you've made of things around here," Pythias allowed, "I'd say that's a pretty apt description."

Sarah felt, rather than heard, a low growl emanating from deep inside Ronald, but the Visitor said nothing.

"Are you all right, Sarah?" Pythias asked.

"Yes."

Pythias nodded. He didn't like the idea of letting Ronald take her, but there was nothing else he could do. As long as she was alive, there was hope, but if Ronald made good his escape and took her with him, she would end up as a meal for a bunch of lizards.

"Throw down your weapons," Ronald said.

They did as he said.

"Go." Ronald nudged Willie with the barrel of his laser.

Willie started forward, Ronald pushing Sarah just behind him. They walked a gauntlet of angry citizens, the people of Cutter's Cove who had come out to fight Ronald and now stood mute as he got away.

Ronald and his two captives were soon in the woods. The alien captain clucked in satisfaction, not even bothering to look behind him. He was certain they wouldn't follow. These foolish humans, drowning in sentiment, unable to sacrifice a single, insignificant life even for the good of the many. Ronald was glad that he had sprung forth from a race that prided itself on its logic.

He was still angry that he had not been able to force Willie to hate him. The would-be philosopher-theologian still talked, though irrationally. He had been seduced by the myth of the apes of ancient times. A session or two in a conversion chamber would straighten him out.

It was awkward going through the woods, but at last they came to the beach. There, on the narrow strip of sand, rested the skyfighter, a pale vulture in the dying sun.

"Get aboard," he said. "We are leaving this place— but first, the formula."

Chapter 47

Ronald made a subvocal command, inaudible to all but the ship's sensors. A hatch opened in the side of the skyfighter, the ramp sliding down, buzzing over the lapping of the waves.

Willie marched disconsolately up the ramp and entered the skyfighter. He collapsed onto a bench, physically exhausted but determined not to let Ronald break his spirit.

"Can you pilot this vehicle?" Ronald asked.

"Yes," Willie said.

"Go to the console then."

Willie did as he was told, running his claws over a panel which lit up in response to his movements.

The engines hummed.

"As soon as the engines are ready, you will take us into the village," Ronald said.

"The village?"

"Yes, to this woman's dwelling. We shall soon see if *she* tells the truth."

Willie waited as long as he reasonably could for the engines to warm up. He knew Sarah was bluffing, and it was only a matter of time until Ronald discovered that she had the last of the toxin secreted on her person. The way he was holding her, she would never get a chance to get the vial out of her pocket. Their only hope now was the toxin, but Ronald never took the laser away from Sarah's head.

"You're wasting time, Willie," Ronald said.

Willie sighed, touching a red light on the panel. The skyfighter lifted gently off the ground and was soon hovering over the tree tops.

At an altitude of a hundred meters, Willie turned the skyfighter toward shore. It shot forward, covering the distance in seconds.

As the water raced underneath them, Sarah grew more and more fearful. What would she do when they reached the house? Would he believe her if she claimed someone else must have got to the toxin first? Her mother, perhaps? Or Pythias Day?

No, he would never swallow a story like that. He was far too cynical. If only he would let go of her, she would be able to think more clearly.

They were over Cutter's Cove now, the church and cemetery below. Willie slowed the skyfighter. "You will have to show me your home, Sarah," he said.

"I'll have to get closer to that screen," she said, hoping Ronald would release her for that purpose.

Instead, he moved closer himself, his taloned hand still around her throat. He was taking no chances.

"On the street," Sarah said. "That house with the tree in front of it."

Willie maneuvered the skyfighter until it was over the street in front of the house, and then he brought it down on the pavement. He entered one last command, and then the engines shut down.

"Outside," Ronald commanded.

The hatch opened, the ramps sliding down to the cracked asphalt. Willie again led the way, stumbling down the ramp and waiting for Ronald and Sarah.

"This house?" Ronald demanded.

"No, this one over here." At least she knew her mother wasn't home.

They went up the steps onto the porch.

"I don't have my key," Sarah said.

Ronald growled impatiently and smashed a small window set in the door. He reached inside and twisted the door handle. The door swung open, and they went inside.

The house was dark, a relief for both Willie and Ronald, but not for Sarah. She tried to snap on a light, but Ronald yanked her away from the switch.

"I see better in the dark," he said. "Now, where is the toxin?"

"It's—ah, it's in the den." Sarah pointed at a darkened doorway at the end of the hall. "In a desk."

Ronald pushed her toward the den, hungrily anticipating victory in spite of all that had happened today. Once he had the toxin, he would be forgiven for losing all his soldiers. They were, after all, expendable. The toxin was not.

There was a big captain's desk set against one wall, a wooden chair set neatly with it.

"Open it," Ronald commanded.

"I don't have the key."

Ronald pointed his laser at the roll top and seared away the varnished wood.

"Open it," he repeated.

Sarah put her hands on the smoldering, smoking wood. Even now, Ronald held her throat firmly so that she could make no sudden moves.

"Ouch!" The embers burned her fingers.

"Open it!" Ronald bellowed.

Sarah flung open the desk.

Willie began to chant as Ronald cast her aside so that he could rummage through the desk. He crumpled papers, pulled out drawers, and tossed them impatiently on the floor. When he saw that there was nothing resembling a chemical formula, he turned angrily to Sarah, the infernal chanting in his ears.

"Where is the toxin?" he demanded.

Sarah held something up, a sparkling little vial.

"Right here," she said, and threw it in Ronald's face.

Chapter 48

Ronald stood perfectly still. Willie chanted, but it was not the same as the chant he had sung before. Now Ronald recognized it as the chant of the dead, apart of the ritual of Zon he had not heard since he was a tiny eggling.

He lifted a hand to his dripping face. Could this virtually tasteless, odorless fluid really be what he had come here for? What so many had died for? It hardly seemed possible.

After all, he felt no ill effect save a slight itching sensation in his mouth. But that could have just been a coincidence, couldn't it? Then the itching turned to fire, and he knew he was lost.

"You!" he shrieked, pointing his laser at Sarah. "You have lied to me!"

"You said there are many truths," Sarah reminded him.

Enraged, Ronald attempted to point the laser at her, but he suffered a terrible spasm at that moment, doubling him over.

The spasm passed, and he tried to lift the laser again, but his paralyzed hand would not respond to his mental command. The figures of Willie and Sarah, so clearly illuminated in the moonlight, began to grow dim.

Another spasm ripped through him, this one much worse than the first. The gun dropped from his numb talons, clattering on the floor.

He was vaguely aware of Sarah picking it up, but he

no longer cared what happened. He was consumed by an ague, frozen and burning up at the same time.

It hardly seemed to matter that he crashed into the desk and sent it tumbling to the floor, his body helplessly following it. He lay there trembling until another spasm wracked him from head to toe. He writhed amid the papers and flames as the sparks from the smoldering desk ignited the contents of the desk spilled onto the floor.

Ronald's tongue flew out of his maw uncontrollably, black bile running down from his jaws onto his crimson uniform. He suddenly understood that he was dying, and what that meant.

All the time, he could hear Willie chanting. But it didn't annoy him as it had in the past. He began to perceive a certain beauty in it now, a soothing accompaniment to this final act of his life.

He rolled through the burning papers, writhing and gagging, and yet his mind calmed even as his body suffered. He had sent so many to their deaths, always fearing it himself, and yet, now that death was upon him, it didn't seem as bad as he had feared.

Soon there would be an end to his suffering, the torment he had known all his life. He began to feel at peace for the first time.

Willie continued to chant as Ronald grew still at last. Sarah stamped out the burning letters and bills on the floor, fearing that the house would burn down. She had the fire under control in a few seconds.

Willie's chanting reached a higher pitch and then trailed off into an ending.

There was silence throughout the house.

"Quickly," Willie said, "we must take his body to the skyfighter."

"Why?" Sarah asked, physically and emotionally drained.

"Please," Willie implored, "help me."

Tired as she was, Sarah didn't like having Ronald's body in the house. "All right."

They awkwardly pulled the body through the dark corridor and out through the front door.

"We must hurry," Willie said.

Sarah didn't understand why, but she took his word for it. She only wanted this nightmare to end.

They dragged the body out into the darkened street. There was nobody in sight, only a single hissing cat under a streetlamp.

Willie and Sarah strained to carry the limp corpse up the ramp. Lungs heaving with their exertions, they finally got Ronald inside.

Willie placed the body at the control console. He chanted for a few seconds and then made a sign in the air over Ronald's head. He turned on the engines.

"Now we must go," he said.

He grabbed Sarah's hand, and they ran out into the street.

"Why are we running?" Sarah asked.

"Just before we debarked, I set the engines to overload to destroy the ship. That way, Ronald could not have taken the toxin back to my people, even if he had succeeded."

"I'm glad you made that decision, Willie, but doesn't it go against your principles?"

"Better one soldier die than an entire planet," Willie replied.

They hid behind a huge oak tree, watching the skyfighter as they caught their breath.

"He would be over the ocean now, had he won," Willie said. "The end would come now."

A bright orange light emerged from the hatch, a tongue of flame licking out toward the Foley house. The skyfighter's shape changed quickly, and then flew apart, scattering debris in all directions, some of it thudding against the houses along the street. A few windows were shattered, the houses illuminated by the blaze, but no real damage was done.

Sarah and Willie watched the wreckage of the sky-fighter burn until they were joined by Pythias Day and the resistance fighters.

Chapter 49

"It looks as if you've got a clean bill of health, Willie," Sarah said, removing the stethoscope from his chest. "The residual effects of the antitoxin were sufficient to combat the virus even when you came into contact with Ronald's body hours after you swallowed the antitoxin."

Willie climbed off the table where Sarah had been examining him. "Thank you," he said. "Though one does one's best not to fear death, at the same time one must relish life."

"The way you put it is a little confusing, Willie," said Pythias Day, "but I think I agree with that sentiment."

"That goes for me too," Jane said, hugging Willie.

"Let me have a squeeze." Sarah hugged him too.

As much as he liked and admired Willie, Pythias couldn't see embracing him. He extended a hand, and Willie shook it vigorously.

"Thank you, Willie," he said. "We couldn't have done it without you."

"I will kiss you all very much," Willie said.

"You mean you'll *miss* us," Sarah laughed.

"Yes, but I wonder about one thing?"

"What's that, Willie?"

"How will I go back to Los Angeles? I have no pseudo skin to wear."

Everyone laughed. "Don't worry about that, Willie. A special limousine is coming to take you back. Jake and

Charlie offered to give you a lift as far as New York, but we've got something even better."

"Oh?"

"Come on outside and take a look."

The four of them went out into the parking lot. It was a sunny day, and the cliff on which Brunk Laboratories sat showed a clear view of the Atlantic sparkling in the morning light.

"It's still beautiful," Jane said. "And it's still ours."

"The fight will continue," Willie cautioned. "My people do not give up so easily."

"I think Ronald was living proof of that," Sarah said. "For a while there, I was beginning to wonder if we were going to make it."

A low hum announced the arrival of Willie's "limousine." They looked up to see a skyfighter descending into the lab parking lot.

"Ah, one of the highjacked craft the resistance maintains," Willie said. "Very good."

As the ramp extended to the asphalt, Willie turned and held out his fingers in a splayed farewell gesture.

"Willie," Sarah said, "I have to know one thing. Why did you destroy Ronald's body and the skyfighter?"

"The skyfighter's destruction was irreversible," Willie replied. "Once the engines were turned on again, the passenger was doomed. As for Ronald, I did it in honor of the *ninj-ki-ra*, which was his religion, just as the *preta-na-ma* is mine."

Though they could have used the body for research, they all understood why Willie had acted as he had. His convictions were very strong.

"Do what you must to end the fighting," Willie said, "so that your world may live in peace."

"I'm looking forward to that day, Willie," said Pythias. "I'm going to retire and write a cookbook."

They all smiled and waved good-bye.

Willie entered the skyfighter, the hatch closed behind him, and the craft lifted off the asphalt.

Caught in sharp relief against a cloud, the skyfighter turned and headed southwest.

Pythias, Jane, and Sarah watched it until it disappeared over the horizon, and then they walked back to Pythias' jeep for the ride down the cliff to their home.

Watch for

DEATH TIDE

next in the **V** series
from Pinnacle Books

coming in July!

DOCTOR WHO

More bestselling science fiction from Pinnacle, America's #1 series publisher!

Join Pinnacle in the fight against illiteracy!